DATE DUE

JUN 08 2012			

CABIN ON TROUBLE CREEK

Jean Van Leeuwen

Dial Books for Young Readers
New York

Published by Dial Books for Young Readers
A division of Penguin Young Readers Group
345 Hudson Street
New York, New York 10014
Copyright © 2004 by Jean Van Leeuwen
All rights reserved
Designed by Jasmin Rubero
Text set in Bembo
Printed in the U.S.A. on acid-free paper

1 3 5 7 9 10 8 6 4 2

Library of Congress Cataloging-in-Publication Data
Van Leeuwen, Jean.
Cabin on Trouble Creek / Jean Van Leeuwen.
p. cm.
Summary: In 1803 in Ohio, two young brothers are left
to finish the log cabin and guard the land while their father
goes back to Pennsylvania to fetch their mother and younger siblings.
ISBN 0-8037-2548-5
[1. Frontier and pioneer life—Ohio—Fiction.
2. Self-reliance—Fiction. 3. Brothers—Fiction.
4. Ohio—History—19th century—Fiction.] I. Title.
PZ7.V3273 Cab 2004
[Fic]—dc22   2003014151

*To Phyllis
for her pioneering spirit
and with thanks
for generous support and encouragement
through the years*

AUGUST

1

Daniel thought his eyes must be playing tricks on him. Those trees. Why, they must be the granddaddies of all the trees in the world. Thick around and tall, with vines growing up their sides as wide as tree trunks themselves. And crowded so tight together, they pretty near blocked out the sky. Never had he seen trees like this back in Pennsylvania.

"Pa," he said, blinking.

But his pa was too busy to pay him any mind. He'd stopped the packhorse, old Ben, and was looking around for something. Old Ben seemed grateful to rest after plodding along since first light. He bent his thin gray neck to browse the forest floor. Daniel's brother Will sat down to rest on a fallen log, then jumped up again as Pa spoke.

"It's here, boys!" he exclaimed. "The mark I made showing our land."

Pa ran his hand over a faint slash in the bark of the biggest tree Daniel had seen yet. This one was so broad around, he thought, it would take five men Pa's size to span its trunk.

"Now," said Pa, "we need to find three more marks like it."

He picketed old Ben so he wouldn't wander. Then they began tramping through the woods, looking for the slashes that would show the boundaries of the land Pa had picked out and paid for last spring.

It was hard walking. Rain had fallen during the night, and the forest floor was soft and spongy under Daniel's feet. There was no trail. They had to climb over waist-high, moss-covered logs and through dense, scratchy thickets. And though it was only mid-afternoon, the woods were dark with a strange green light. Somewhere up above the treetops was the sun, but its beams could not poke through the thick canopy of leaves.

You could get lost in woods like these, Daniel thought. Each tree looked so much like the next one, and they stood so close together. Like the long, thick, scarred legs of some giant beast. There was something unfriendly about these looming trees, unwelcoming. It was as if they were saying, *This is our land. You have no place here.*

But what bothered Daniel even more was the quiet. Not a rustle, not a birdsong, not a flash of squirrel leaping among the branches overhead. Seemed like nothing was alive here.

Or maybe something was. Some wild creature stalking them, waiting to spring. Like wolves. Or a bear. Or even a panther. Pa said all of them lived in this vast woods that was now, in the year 1803, called the new state of Ohio.

Probably not Indians, though. Most of the Delawares and Shawnees and Monsees had moved on to the north and west.

What was that? Just behind him Daniel heard a small sound. Like something creeping stealthily through the brush. He whirled around, his heart thumping loudly in his chest. And saw the waving gray tail of a squirrel disappearing around the side of a tree.

Daniel let out a long breath of relief. At the same time he felt a prick of shame for being afraid. He was eleven years old, after all. He looked over to see if Will had been frightened. But his brother didn't appear to have noticed. Though Will was just nine, he never seemed scared of anything. He darted quickly through the trees, circling their trunks to look for the signs Pa had left. A moment later, he vanished from sight.

"Stay close, boy," Pa warned in his deep, growling voice. He too must be thinking about the chance of getting lost.

It was Will who found the next slash mark.

"Pa!" he shouted. "Look here!"

Pa ran his hand over another long cut in the rough bark of an elm tree. He nodded. "That's it."

He sighted through the trees. "Should be a creek over thereabouts," he told them, "if I recollect right."

They heard it before they saw it, a thin ripple of sound. Then the trees opened up a little and Daniel made out the glint of running water. Moments later, the three of them stood on the bank of a wide stream, deep and slow-moving, with bits of leaves and twigs drifting on top like tiny canoes on a river. Daniel and Will peered into the water for fish. Daniel couldn't see any, but he'd bet plenty were hiding in that dark water.

"Man I bought the land from said they call this Trouble Creek," Pa said. "Seems there was a massacre hereabouts a few years back."

"A massacre?" Daniel swallowed hard.

"A band of Indians ambushed a party of white soldiers up from Virginia. Killed them all. Started a big bunch of trouble."

Looking into the water, Daniel suddenly saw a reddish color. Blood. But that was foolish. Whatever had happened years ago had long since been washed away by the stream.

"We've got nothing to fear," Pa added quickly. "Things have been peaceful in these parts close to ten years now."

Peaceful. That was how the creek looked to Daniel, with its gently flowing water and curling ferns, a pair of dragonflies hovering over its mossy bank. It was hard to imagine anything bad had ever happened here.

Pa gazed down at the earth under their feet. "Just look at this soil, boys," he said, poking a stick into it. "Black as charcoal. Soil like this will grow anything."

He hunted around the bank till he found a slash on a buttonwood tree that leaned across the creek to meet another on the opposite side. After that Pa seemed pretty certain where the fourth one was. He led them upstream, struggling through low bushes and sliding across muddy places, until finally they found the last marked tree.

Pa looked around him with satisfaction.

"It's a good parcel of land," he declared. "Flat for growing fields, water nearby but not swampy. We'll not have to worry about fever and ague. We can make a farm here."

A farm. Here in the midst of these giant trees. Daniel tried to conjure up a picture of it in his mind, but it wouldn't come clear. Back in Pennsylvania there were woods, all right, but also beautiful valleys with fields and open spaces. And neighbors just down the road. No neighbors would be just down the road here. There was no road. And no one living closer, Pa had said, than fifteen miles. This state of Ohio was nothing but one huge, unending forest.

"Pa," he said slowly. "What about all the trees?"

Pa looked at him. His eyes, small in his broad, weathered face, looked tired. His jaw, though, was firm. Stubborn, that was what some folks back home called Pa. Just for a moment, in the dim green light, he reminded Daniel of one of the sturdy, tough-skinned trees standing all around them.

"We'll chop them down," he said.

2

They started the next day.

First thing they needed, Pa said, was a lean-to for shelter till they got their cabin built. He took his axe and cut down some thin saplings. He found two with forked branches and stuck the ends into the ground, laying a crosspiece between. Along this crosspiece, Daniel and Will piled more saplings sloping down to the ground. Then they stacked up brush on the sides and more on top. By mid-morning, they had a three-sided shelter to keep off the rain. It was barely big enough for the three of them, and Pa couldn't quite sit upright, but he said it would do.

Pa rolled a fair-sized log across the front. He gathered together some dry leaves and twigs, struck a spark with his flint on a bit of charred cloth, and blew on it until it smoked and finally burst into a tiny red flame.

"We'll keep a fire going day and night," he told them. "That will scare off any woods varmints."

Though they scarcely needed it for warmth these late-summer days, Daniel was glad for the fire between them and whatever creatures might be out there among the trees.

He and Will emptied out the packs old Ben had carried, and lined up their supplies at the front of the lean-to. The large sack of cornmeal, the small one of salt. A few potatoes. A near-empty jug of molasses. The big iron pot and the smaller frying pan. Her spider, Ma called it, on account of its sitting up on three legs in the fire. If Ma was here, Daniel thought, she'd have this rough lean-to cozied up so it felt like home in no time at all. But Ma was back in Pennsylvania, waiting for the cabin to be finished before she and the four little ones joined them.

His little sister Sarah, just turned six, and Abby, five. They did everything together. Zeke, only three but trying to do whatever Daniel and Will did, falling down and scrambling right up again. And the new baby born in the early summer. Josiah, he was called, after Pa's oldest brother.

Could be Pa was thinking of them too. He stopped only to eat some cold johnnycake before picking up his axe again.

"I have in mind a likely spot for our cabin," he told Daniel and Will.

Once more the two boys followed him through the trees. Elm, oak, and sugar maple, Daniel saw. Beech, walnut, hickory, and here and there a slender dogwood. Those were only some of the trees in this unending forest. Others Daniel hadn't come across before and didn't know their names. Pa took them to a small rise not far from the creek.

"Here," he said.

It was a likely spot, Daniel thought. Ma would be happy not to have to walk far to fetch water for cooking and washing. Yet it was high enough to stay dry when spring rains came. Not only that, but Pa pointed out a spring of pure drinking water flowing out of a little mossy place nearby.

Daniel cupped some into his hand and drank. It was icy cold and smelled of some sweet herb. Ma would know which one. She would gather it and all the other herbs in these woods for tonics and cures when she came.

Without another word, Pa began swinging his axe at the trees.

He picked out a good-sized oak and cut a notch in its side. Daniel knew this was the side where he wanted it to fall. Then Pa set back on his heels and let his axe fly. He swung from his feet, all his strength flowing up and out through the head of the axe. Pa was not a tall man, nor did he look real powerful. But when he swung his axe, Daniel was amazed. Suddenly he had the grace and power of a giant.

Time after time the axe head bit into the dark tree trunk, cutting a deep, bright-colored wound. Until at last Daniel heard the oak creak.

"Stand clear, boys!" Pa shouted.

The tree leaned. It swayed. It seemed to shudder. Then, very slowly, it toppled and fell with a muffled crash.

"Hurrah!" cheered Will.

The oak lay on the ground, massive and still. Its broken limbs sprawled out in all directions, some leaning against the trees next to it, others reaching down nearly to the creek. Yet, looking up, Daniel saw no difference in the wall of trees around them.

He and Will set to work, rolling away and hauling off as much of the stripped-off branches and brush as they could. Pa did not stop to rest, but went on to the next tree, a tall, straight elm. Once more his axe swung strong and true, carving a deeper and deeper slice into the tree's side.

"Stand clear!" Pa's voice rang out again. Daniel heard that terrible creaking sound, and the elm too came crashing down.

By late afternoon a tumble of fallen trees covered the ground. But still Daniel could not make out any hole in the dark green ceiling overhead. They had not made a clearing.

Not yet. Pa would not quit, though. He never would quit. He would attack those trees again tomorrow, Daniel knew.

Back at the lean-to, Daniel was glad to sit down. But Pa still would not rest. He picked up his musket and said, "I'll see what I can find us for supper."

Will's face brightened. "Can I come too?" he asked. He loved to hunt. At home he was in the woods as much as Ma would let him, shooting birds and squirrels and rabbits.

Pa shook his head. "You boys build up the fire. Have the kettle ready to boil when I get back."

Will's face fell, but he didn't say any more. If Daniel told him to do something, he'd be sure to argue. But you didn't argue with Pa. When he made up his mind to something, his face turned hard. It was no use trying to sway him.

In just a few steps Pa was gone, swallowed up by the shadowy trees. Their towering trunks seemed to press closer around the lean-to as daylight faded and quiet settled over the woods again. And once more Daniel felt a sharp little prickle inside his chest. What if something should happen to Pa? What if he didn't come back? What would they do?

Will didn't seem to have these kinds of thoughts. Already he was busy poking at the fire with a long stick. As the coals began to glow, Will fed them with bits of dry twigs. Soon little flames were licking upward.

A good fire was what they needed, Daniel thought. Fire would keep away the woods varmints. Keep the three of them safe. He hurried to gather fallen branches to feed the flames. And even after their fire was burning bright and steady, he kept piling more dead wood next to the lean-to.

By the time Pa returned, water was beginning to bubble in the iron pot.

He dropped a small bundle on the ground.

"Rabbit," he said with a rare smile.

Daniel skinned it, cutting the meat into chunks with his knife and dropping it into the pot. Soon the lean-to was filled with the good smell of rabbit stew. It made him think again of Ma. Of course her rabbit stew would be full of other savory things: wild mushrooms, onions, carrots, a pinch of this or that herb from her garden. Still, this plain stew smelled mighty fine.

When they finished eating it, mopping out the pot with the last scraps of johnnycake, the three of them stretched out to sleep.

There was just room enough in the lean-to for them to lie side by side, if no one rolled over. And Pa's feet about reached the fire.

"'Night, boys," he said. In a minute he was breathing deeply.

Daniel felt snug lying between Pa and Will in the tight little shelter they had built. His stomach was full of rabbit stew. The fire still flickered brightly between him and the dark, towering trees.

He was about to doze off when he heard the sound.

Ah-oooooh. It was eerie, a slowly rising cry that went on and on, then hung in the air like something not of this world.

Now it came again, from a different part of the forest. Long, drawn out, and mournful. It sent a shiver creeping up his spine.

Daniel clutched at Pa's arm till he came awake with a start.

"What is it?" Pa sat up on his elbows, reaching for his gun. Then he lay back down. "Wolves," he said.

So it was true there were wolves in this forest. Inside his head Daniel could see them, lifting their sharp noses to howl at the night sky. Gray, ghostlike shapes circling closer and closer through the trees.

"It's all right," Pa told him, his voice softer. "They won't attack us. They only go after the weak and the wounded. And we have our fire."

Daniel stared into the fire's red glow. That fire was a comfort, no doubt about it. It warmed him outside and in.

In a moment Pa went off to sleep again. And finally Daniel did too. But in his dreams, gray ghostlike shapes floated among the trees, their unearthly cries echoing in the night.

3

It took days to make a small clearing. Long, hard days with the sound of Pa's axe ringing out in the quiet forest from first light to near dusk. Daniel and Will worked alongside him, lifting and carrying, pushing and rolling. When they got back to the lean-to, they were both so tired, they fell asleep almost before finishing their supper of rabbit or squirrel.

In Daniel's dreams now, all he saw was the flash of the axe head slicing into raw wood. Over and over and over again. And all he heard was the crash of falling trees.

A few of the trees Pa didn't cut down outright. Those were the granddaddy trees, the ones that looked like they'd been there since the start of creation. He cut deep gashes all around their enormous gnarled trunks. Girdling, he called it. The cuts deadened the trees, not letting the sap rise up to the leaves. The leaves would turn yellow, and in a few months those great trees would wither and die.

Little by little, Pa's axe did its work. The gloom of the woods slowly began to lift. One day, glancing up at the treetops, Daniel made out a tiny, shifting patch of blue sky.

"Pa!" he said. "Look there."

Pa barely paused swinging his axe. "Yep," he grunted. "Could be we've made some headway."

The straightest trees Pa cut into lengths for the cabin walls. Daniel and Will hitched up old Ben to drag them to the spot where the cabin would stand. The longer logs would become the front and back walls, the shorter ones the two ends. Day by day, the piles grew higher.

Looking at them, Daniel thought surely they had enough logs now to build a cabin.

But Pa shook his head. "We'll need about eighty logs in all," he said.

He moved away from the clearing, searching the woods for likely trees. Will wandered with him. His voice rang out from all over.

"Here's a good one!

"Pa, look over here!"

Finally Pa was satisfied that he had enough. Picking two of the stoutest timbers, he laid them out on the ground where the cabin was to stand. With his axe, he cut notches in each end. Then, from the pile of shorter logs, he selected two more and notched them just the same. With Daniel's and Will's help, he laid these across the first two, matching notch to notch. They fit together neat as could be. Pa stood back and eyed them to make sure the corners were square.

"There," he said. "We've got the start of a cabin."

Pa cut notches in four more logs. With Daniel and Will

on one end and Pa on the other, they lifted them into place on top of the first ones. The logs were not even, and Daniel could see daylight between them. But he knew they'd be chinking those cracks later and daubing them with clay to keep out the rain and snow.

By the end of the afternoon, they had cabin walls four logs high.

It got harder after that. Lifting the heavy logs made Daniel's back ache. And though Will never would complain, his face grew red and Daniel saw his thin arms shaking with strain.

Pa gave them a few minutes' rest.

"I could wish we had neighbors to help out," he admitted. "We're a little shorthanded."

Nothing could be done about that. So Pa devised a different way of lifting the logs into place. He dragged over two long, straight tree limbs, resting one end on the ground and the other on the log wall. They rolled the logs up this rough ramp, then Pa set them in their notches.

Slowly the walls grew taller. Higher than Daniel's head, higher than Pa's. They had to use forked poles cut from saplings to help move the highest logs into place. Until finally, a few days later, the walls were finished. Pa cut an opening in the front wall for a door and another, on one end, for a fireplace.

"You boys go down to the creek and look for stones," he ordered. "Big ones, to build the fireplace wall."

Back and forth to the creek went Daniel and Will, hauling the heavy stones. Meanwhile, Pa moved on to the roof. He had saved out one long, straight log. This he stretched from one built-up end of the cabin to the other. Then he laid down sapling poles like ribs, forming a skeleton of a roof. With the ribs lashed in place, he began covering them with slabs of bark stripped from elm and basswood trees.

"I daresay it will leak," he said, "but it will have to do for now. Maybe come spring we can put on a clapboard roof."

When the boys had piled up all the large stones they could find, Pa sent them back to the creek to mix up the mud that would hold the fireplace together.

"Look for clay along the banks," he told them.

As usual, it was Will whose sharp eyes spotted the streaks of white in the dark earth overhanging the creek.

"There!" he said. "Oh, and over there!"

Daniel felt a little prick of annoyance. Why was it Will seemed ahead of him all the time? He was the oldest. He ought to be the leader.

He tried to make his voice sound like Pa's. "We'll poke it out with sticks," he told Will.

Daniel started digging out the clay.

"I see more on the other side!" exclaimed Will.

Before Daniel could answer, Will took a running start and leaped for the opposite bank. Looking up, Daniel saw him teetering on the edge over the dark, running water.

For a second, it looked like he would fall in. Then he grabbed a rock and pulled himself up.

"Did it!" He scrambled up, clutching his ankle.

"Are you hurt?" Daniel asked.

"Not much." Will grinned.

"Why'd you do that? You could have waded across."

"Just wanted to see if I could."

That was Will. Not thinking about getting hurt. Just wanting to see if he could.

"Pa's waiting," Daniel reminded him.

They poked out the clay and mixed it with water in the bucket until they had a thick mud. Then Daniel carried the bucket back to the cabin. Will was limping a little, he noticed.

Stone by stone, Pa showed them how to build a three-sided fireplace around the opening he had left for it. Will lined up stones on the ground outside the cabin. Daniel covered the tops and sides with the clay mixture, filling in all the cracks as smooth and even as he could. Will set on more stones and Daniel plastered them over. Now and then they had to stop to mix up more mud at the creek.

Just like the log walls, the fireplace rose higher and higher. Until they ran out of stones.

"What should we do?" Daniel asked Pa.

The fireplace was only as high as his chin, and it needed to go all the way up to the roof.

Pa stopped his work to look it over.

19

"We'll leave it for now," he decided. "Before winter comes, we can finish it off with a stick-and-clay chimney."

Pa wasn't one not to complete a job he had started. He'd never let Daniel or Will quit any task till they'd done every last bit just right. For sure, he was in a hurry, Daniel thought. They needed to finish the cabin before the days turned cool. And maybe too it was on account of Ma. Ever since this last baby came, she'd been feeling poorly, sitting down to rest after every chore. Most likely Pa was thinking about getting home to her.

He worked hard all the next day to finish the roof, while Daniel and Will cleaned up inside the cabin. They piled leftover chips of wood next to the fireplace. Daniel turned over a fat end of tree trunk to make a rough chair to sit on. Will found another like it, and they rolled it inside. Finally, they hunted around in the brush for dry leaves. Combing out the twigs, they piled up the leaves along one wall for beds.

It was late afternoon by the time they finished.

Pa set down his axe next to the door.

"Well," he said, looking around. "Looks like we can move in."

So they brought everything from the lean-to and arranged it near the fireplace. The meal sack and the salt bag and other supplies. The iron pot and frying pan. Just one wooden spoon, and no dishes. They hadn't had room in the saddlebags for anything more. Pa hung up a blanket over the doorway.

"I'll bring some nails when I come back to make a proper door," he said. "We'll lay down a puncheon floor and build a sleeping loft. And no doubt your ma will want a window."

Of course she would. For Ma, a house without a window or two wouldn't be civilized.

And Pa would build a table, Daniel thought, and benches or three-legged stools to sit on. Pa was handy with tools. Later on, for sure, there would be real bedsteads, and shelves for Ma's dishes. Maybe even a cupboard in the corner.

"Let's see how you boys did with the fireplace," Pa said.

Would it draw? Daniel wondered. Had they built it high enough and sealed the stones tight enough?

He and Will brought in some dry twigs and larger sticks of wood and laid them out in the fireplace opening. Pa struck a spark into a pile of leaves and bark. They flamed up, spreading the fire to the wood.

Smoke came billowing out, stinging Daniel's eyes.

Pa frowned. Will began to cough. Smoke kept pouring out, filling the cabin with a gray haze.

The fireplace wasn't going to work.

Then one of the large sticks of wood caught fire. The smoke started going up instead of out. And little by little, the haze cleared.

"Looks like it's going to draw all right," said Pa. "You boys built that fireplace good and stout."

21

It was rare that Pa praised anything they did. Daniel looked over at Will. His brother always wore his feelings right on his face. Sure enough, Will's mouth split into a wide grin.

Daniel felt the same, though he kept it inside.

He looked around the cabin in the flickering firelight. The log walls felt tight around them. The leafy beds had a fresh, clean smell. The bulging sack of meal in the corner promised that they wouldn't go hungry.

Just for that moment, Daniel didn't see the cracks between the logs and the unfinished door and the roof that was sure to leak. Instead, he saw it as it would be. Ma bending over a bubbling stew at the fireplace. Pa on a bench nearby, oiling his musket. He and Will showing Zeke how to whittle a whistle from a hollowed-out bit of wood. The little girls setting the table for supper while the baby rocked peacefully in his cradle.

The family together again, snug in their cabin. Soon.

SEPTEMBER

4

Pa left two days later. He swung one leg over old Sam's back and pulled himself up in the saddle. He sat there for a long moment, looking down at Daniel and Will.

"Now, you boys know what to do while I'm gone," he said. "Work on chinking and daubing the cabin walls like I told you. Cut sticks to build the chimney and stack up firewood. You've got plenty of meal. I'll be back with Ma and the little ones in five weeks' time. Six at the outside."

"Yes, Pa," said Daniel.

"We'll have the whole cabin done," promised Will.

"And don't let your fire go out," Pa cautioned.

"No, Pa," said Daniel.

For a moment, Pa seemed to hesitate. Maybe, Daniel thought, he was having second thoughts about leaving them alone. But that had been the plan, the one they'd talked about so many nights around the fire ever since last spring. The boys would work on readying the cabin while Pa went back to Pennsylvania to fetch the rest of the family.

They wouldn't be alone for long. Besides, Daniel was going on twelve years old. He was nearly grown. He drew himself up as tall as he could.

"Tell Ma we'll have the cabin ready for her," he said.

Pa nodded, looking at him with those eyes that could bore a hole right through you. "One more thing. Seeing you're the oldest, Daniel, I'm counting on you to take charge."

Daniel swallowed hard. "Yes, Pa."

Pa shifted his gaze to Will. "You be sure to mind your brother now."

Will looked down at the ground. Daniel thought he knew what his brother was thinking. It was hard for him to mind anyone, specially Daniel.

"You hear me, Will?" Pa's voice was sharp.

"Yes, sir," Will answered softly.

"I best be on my way then," Pa said. He clucked to old Ben, turning the horse's head toward the trees. "So long, boys."

"Bye, Pa."

Daniel stood watching as old Ben ambled away. In an instant, it seemed, his gray shape faded into the forest. And Pa was gone.

Silence surrounded them once more. Daniel heard it loud in his ears. Once again he had the strange feeling that no living creature besides himself and Will inhabited these woods. He strained to hear the smallest sound, but not even a whisper of a breeze rustled the leaves.

Listening, he felt an uneasiness in the pit of his stomach. He and Will were alone now in this wilderness, fifteen miles from any neighbor and not even knowing which way a neighbor might be. They were all alone with the trees. And he was in charge. In charge of finishing the cabin, making it ready for the family. In charge of Will, who was so headstrong, he was likely not to mind him, no matter what he'd promised Pa. In charge of feeding the two of them and keeping them safe.

He wished Pa hadn't taken his gun. But the old musket Pa had used ever since his days in the Continental Army was the only gun they had. Besides, it had gotten so cantankerous, Pa said, that Daniel would as likely shoot his foot off as any game he was aiming at.

He'd left the axe and two knives. And they had the fire.

I won't let the fire go out, Daniel told himself. Not ever.

"Aren't you coming?"

Will, the water bucket in his hand, was starting for the creek. "Pa said to daub the cabin walls," he reminded Daniel.

That was the thing to do. Get right to work. Keeping busy left you no time to think.

"I'm coming," said Daniel.

Will never stopped talking while they dug up more clay, mixed it with water, and carried it back to the cabin.

"Is that a fish?" He pointed at a ripple in the stream. "Bet I could catch one. Tomorrow I'm going to try.

"See those streaks of clay on the other bank? If we had another bucket, I'd wade over and fill it.

27

"Wish Pa had left his gun. I'd shoot us a squirrel for supper."

Daniel didn't mind Will's chatter. It filled up the silence of the woods.

Pa had showed them before he left how to chink the widest spaces in the cabin walls where ribbons of daylight came streaming in. With the axe, Daniel lopped off a good-sized splinter of wood and trimmed it to fit the space. Then the two boys daubed clay all around it till the opening was sealed. After that, they used the clay to fill in the smaller cracks between logs.

It seemed strange not to have Pa looking over their shoulders, telling them what to do next. Or answering their questions. Should he fit the wedges of wood tighter between the logs? Daniel wondered. Was their clay mixture too wet to hold?

Right or wrong, he realized, he was going to have to decide on his own. Pa had said so. He was the oldest. He was in charge. He was going to have to act like Pa.

The work went slowly. It was hard shaping the little pieces of chinking wood with the axe so they fit snugly between logs. Sometimes Daniel ruined one and had to start over. Once he nicked his hand. And Will had to keep going back to the creek for more clay. By late afternoon, they had only filled in the cracks between the three bottom logs on the north side.

It wasn't much. Not nearly as much as Daniel had hoped for. Still, he thought they'd done a pretty fair job.

He stood back to look. Before, they'd been able to see between those logs straight to the outside. And when it got colder, the wind would blow through and the rain and snow would come seeping in. Now the light was blocked out. He couldn't make out a single speck of daylight.

If Pa was here, he'd be pleased, Daniel thought. "No use doing a job unless you do it right," he always said. It felt good to think they had done the job right.

And if Pa was here, he'd be sure to keep them working till the light failed. But Daniel's shoulders ached so, he could barely lift the axe.

He was in charge now. He could decide.

"We'll quit now for supper," he told Will.

Daniel set down the axe just inside the door, like Pa did every night. Will began poking at the coals in the fireplace. Then Daniel mixed up some cornmeal with water and baked it on a slab of wood turned toward the fire. They ate their johnnycake along with what was left of last night's squirrel stew.

Most likely they wouldn't be having squirrel or rabbit for supper after this. But they could make do for five weeks. Maybe Will really would catch fish in the creek to go with their johnnycake. Knowing him, he was bound to try. They could look for berries too, and for nuts later on.

With his stomach pleasantly full, Daniel sat on his log chair looking into the fire. It was surprising how different he felt from when Pa had left this morning. He and Will had put in a good day's work. Even without Pa telling them what to do, nothing had gone wrong. Though it was still a little smoky, the fireplace they had built worked. And they had the start of a good, tight cabin. If he and Will worked hard every day on the chinking and daubing, they could easily have it finished by the time Pa returned. Maybe they could even do more.

"Could be," he said out loud, "we'll surprise Pa and have a floor put in when he gets back."

Will looked up, his eyes bright in the firelight.

"And the chimney all finished off," he added.

"Could be," said Daniel.

5

The days continued to be warm, though the nights were beginning to cool off. The boys soon fell into a routine. Up at first light, uncovering the coals in the fireplace, adding wood to get a good blaze going. Then a bit of johnnycake, or sometimes a pot of hot cornmeal mush, with a few drops of molasses from the fast-emptying jug for sweetening. After that, Will would set off for the creek to mix the mud–clay in the bucket, while Daniel picked up the axe.

They worked all day at the chinking and daubing. Then, in the late afternoon, they went foraging for berries and nuts. They found a few dried-up raspberries, the last of the season, in a thicket near the creek, and here and there some wild grapes. And nuts had begun falling from the trees, knocked down by squirrels.

Will darted here and there, almost always the first to spot something.

"Look here!" he would call.

And moments later from somewhere else, "Daniel! Come see what I found!"

Daniel worried that he would wander too far away and get lost in the trees.

"Stay in sight of the cabin or the creek," he warned.

But Will didn't listen. A few minutes later, his voice would come from a different direction.

"I knew I'd find grapes. I could smell them!"

Daniel was grateful for the grapes. Still, it made him uneasy trying to keep track of his brother all the time. Trying to make him mind. It looked like Will had already forgotten what Pa had said before he left.

Will also tried to catch fish in the creek. He had no hook or line or fishing pole. However, that didn't stop him. He stood bent over in the middle of the creek, staring intently into the water. When he caught a glimpse of something moving, his hands darted down.

They came up empty every time. But Will wasn't discouraged.

"I'll make me a fishing spear," he told Daniel.

After their evening meal of johnnycake accompanied by any fruit they had found, the two boys sat on their log chairs close to the fire.

Will worked on sharpening a point in the end of the long straight stick that would be his fishing spear. And Daniel used his knife to do some whittling. First, he made two forks. Encouraged by his success, he went on to carve two rough spoons. Then he decided to try his hand at turning a small chunk of wood into a drinking cup. It took him several nights to get the shape of it. After that, he began hollowing out the inside. Chipping away with just the tip of his knife for a tool was hard work.

They talked about what Pa and Ma were doing.

"They've set out in the wagon by now," Will figured. "Ma and the baby and the girls will be riding and Pa and Zeke walking alongside, with our good old dog Trooper trailing behind. I expect Zeke will want to walk the whole way."

Daniel had to smile at the thought.

"I wonder if Pa traded for a new horse," he said. Pa was afraid old Ben wouldn't make it over those mountains pulling the heavy wagon. "And maybe he'll bring a cow too."

Just thinking about having milk to put on his corn-meal mush made Daniel lick his lips.

"Likely right now they've found shelter for the night in some cabin along the road," Will went on.

"Or they're sleeping under the wagon," said Daniel.

He thought about all the nights he and Pa and Will had camped out on the hard ground with only a thin blanket underneath them. And about the long road running from Philadelphia to Pittsburgh, called a turnpike but hardly a road at all. It was narrow and steep through the mountains, washed out in places and blocked by fallen trees. Rough men along the way charged travelers for clearing the road of timber that Pa said most likely they'd felled themselves. It had been hard enough with just a packhorse, but a wagon would have slow, difficult going. And after that came the trip upriver on a flat boat that might snag on driftwood or go aground.

It would be a long, dangerous journey. Pa would make it through, though, Daniel had no doubt about that. After sharing a farm so long with his older brother, Uncle Isaac, he was determined to have his own land even if he had to take this wild forest and tame it. He and Ma had talked about it nearly as long as Daniel could remember. West was the place to go, Pa said. That was where land was plentiful and cheap. And this past spring, at last, he had come out and found the land he wanted.

Each night, just before lying down on his bed of leaves, Daniel scratched a mark with his knife on the bottom log of the wall next to the fireplace. Counting off the days till Pa returned with the family.

Sixteen marks there were now. Close to halfway, he calculated, if the trip went well.

"Good night," he'd say, rolling up in his blanket.

Sometimes Will answered and sometimes he didn't. Will fell asleep fast and slept hard, the way he did everything.

Daniel often lay awake for a while, listening to the small night sounds. The crackling of the dying fire. Will's deep breathing. Outside, the low hoot of an owl in the trees. And, nearly every night, the howling of wolves.

He'd grown used to the sound now. It was part of the night. As long as the wolves kept their distance, their howling didn't bother him. And he had yet to see one.

Still, Daniel thought, he would be glad when he scratched that last mark on the log beside the fireplace.

6

Will finished his fishing spear. Feeling its sharp point, Daniel had no doubt it would pierce right through any fish.

"Now I'll catch us something for supper," said Will.

Daniel watched as he waded knee-deep into the creek. He stood still, the spear poised in his hand, waiting. For a long time Will didn't move, just stared into the slowly-moving water. Then Daniel saw his shoulder tense. And suddenly his spear struck.

"Ahhh." Will looked at Daniel in disappointment. "It got away."

He tried again. Daniel was surprised at how patient his brother could be, standing so still for so long, until he spotted another fish.

Once more his spear darted down. And once more Will scowled in frustration. "I'm not fast enough," he muttered.

He practiced, thrusting his spear into the water again and again. The clear water turned cloudy.

Daniel thought he must have scared away all the fish by now.

"Maybe you ought to try another spot," he suggested.

Will moved upstream, to where the creek widened to form a roundish pool.

"Most likely the big ones live here," he said, grinning. "Just you wait. We'll have a whole mess of fish for supper tonight."

Thinking of fish sizzling in the frying pan, Daniel felt a stab of hunger. Johnnycake and berries were enough to keep you from starving, but they didn't fill you up the way fish or meat did. He longed for the stews they'd had those nights with Pa. Maybe he could figure a way of catching small animals. But how? Without a gun or traps, it seemed impossible. Anyway, Pa would be back before long and they'd be shooting game again.

Will waded into the quiet pool. He peered into the water, his spear held ready. As patiently as before, he waited.

Daniel knew when he saw a fish. Will's whole body tightened. His wrist lifted slightly. Then his spear stabbed into the water, quick as a lightning strike.

No doubt about it, he'd gotten faster. But still he came up empty. Again and again, the slippery fish swam away too fast.

Once, Will was sure he had something.

"Daniel!" he cried. "I got a big one!"

Excitedly, he pulled up his spear. Then he looked down in disbelief. Stuck on the end was a large, soggy, brown leaf.

Disgusted, Will threw down his spear. Daniel picked it

up. The point was broken, so it was useless to try to fish any more today.

"Come on," he said. "We'll try again tomorrow."

That night Will began working on a new fishing spear. He was like Pa that way, Daniel thought. Once his mind was set on something, he would never give up. He was like Pa in another way too. Pa crafted most of the tools needed on the farm himself. Rakes and scoops and shovels, a plow, a wheelbarrow, a sled. He seemed to know how to do it without anyone showing him how. Will must have been watching all those nights at home around the fire.

His new spear was longer and heavier than the first one. After peeling off the bark, Will carefully shaved off every bump and rough edge till it was straight and smooth. Then he worked on the end. He sharpened it to a fine point and hardened the point by holding it over the fire's hot coals. It took three nights before Will was satisfied.

"It's going to work this time," he told Daniel. "I know it."

The day was cloudy, with the smell of rain. It began to drizzle in the early afternoon, and by the time the boys stopped work on the cabin, the woods were damp and gray.

"Now's the best time for fishing," Will said excitedly, as they walked down the path they'd beaten to the creek over the past weeks.

37

The trees leaned over them, heavy and mossy and dripping. On days like this, Daniel felt like they were crowding in even closer. A dense mist filled the spaces between them, and wet leaves reached out to brush his shirt, making him feel clammy all over.

Will paid no attention to anything but his spear. At the creek he tried it out, making quick stabs into the shallow water. Daniel watched, sitting on a log that lay half in and half out of the water.

"Feels good," Will said.

He waded out and took his stance as before, the new spear held ready to strike. He stood that way a long time, like something rooted and growing there. When Will finally moved, Daniel was startled. The spear darted down and came up.

Empty again.

But Will didn't seem discouraged. He moved a little way downstream. Daniel followed, keeping an eye out for signs of clay on the muddy banks. He was poking a stick into a likely streak of grayish-white when he heard splashing.

"Got him!" cried Will.

He held his spear high in triumph, a wriggling brown fish caught on the end of it. A trout, it looked like. A good-sized one too. Big enough to fill both their bellies for supper tonight.

Will's grin was so wide, Daniel couldn't help smiling himself.

"You were right," he said. "The new spear did it."

Encouraged by his success, Will wanted to keep fishing. But, looking around him, Daniel saw that the gray mist was growing thicker. He could barely make out the trees on the other side of the creek. What if they couldn't find the path back to the cabin? They might get lost in the woods. And darkness would come soon. He knew what Pa would say.

"We better get back," he said, "before we can't see our way."

They tramped upstream to the place where Will had started fishing. Daniel was relieved to see the little clump of ferns he remembered, the log half in and half out of the water. They hadn't lost the path.

"Now that I've got the hang of it," Will said happily, "we'll have fish every night."

He walked along, swinging the fish in one hand, the spear in the other.

"Why, I wager when Pa and Ma get here, I can catch enough for a fish feast," he boasted.

Ahead on the path, Daniel noticed some nuts. Chestnuts, it looked like. The first of those tasty, red-brown nuts of the season. He stooped to pick them up.

Above him he heard a sudden cracking sound.

"Watch out!" cried Will.

A tree limb came crashing down, right at Daniel's feet. Looking up, he saw what had made it fall. A large black shape peered down at him. It had a thick head, a pointed snout, and long, sharp claws.

A bear! All at once he remembered something Pa had told him a long time ago. Bears loved nuts. They would even climb trees to get them. And now this bear was moving, climbing surprisingly fast down the tree.

"Run!" gasped Daniel.

The two boys raced for the cabin, stumbling over tree roots, falling and scrambling up again. Daniel didn't dare look back. He heard loud, raspy breathing. Was it the bear close behind them, crashing through the brush? Or was the noise inside his own head?

He was in the lead, Will close behind. They were in sight of the cabin now. He thought of the axe right inside the cabin door.

"Grab your knife," he told Will. "I'll get the axe."

But where was Will? Suddenly he wasn't behind him.

Daniel looked back. There was Will, running the wrong way. Back toward the bear.

"Will!"

He was out of sight now. And Daniel couldn't see the bear either. He darted in the cabin door, grabbed hold of the axe, and ran out. He stopped short, his knees shaking, not sure what to do.

Then out of the trees came Will, running hard. Daniel couldn't see the bear, but Will was running like it was right on his heels. He jumped over a log, burst through a tangled thicket of bushes, then skidded to a stop by the cabin door.

"My fish!" he gasped. "Dropped it. Had to go back."

40

"You went back for a fish?" Daniel couldn't believe it. "Where's the bear?"

"It started after me, but I got away. I don't think it followed me."

Daniel looked back at the path, scanning the trees. Was there a bear out there somewhere? If so, it was bound to be an angry bear. Wouldn't it make a lot of noise? He heard nothing and saw nothing. Still, the mist made it hard to be sure.

"Come inside," he told Will.

They were both shivering, from their wet clothes or from fear, Daniel wasn't sure which. Maybe both. Will built up the fire while Daniel stood by the door, the axe still in his hand. He stayed there looking out until the mist turned to darkness. Finally he was satisfied that no bear was prowling around outside.

Foolish was the word he kept hearing inside his head. Just plain foolish. That was what Pa would say about Will.

Going back into danger for a fish.

What would Pa tell Will if he was here? How would he make him understand that he could have been killed by that bear? One blow from its powerful paw, and Will wouldn't be sitting here getting ready to fry up his fish for supper.

Daniel wished hard that Pa was here. But he wasn't. There was nothing else for it, Daniel was going to have to talk to Will himself.

He waited until they'd finished their supper and Will

41

was scrubbing out the frying pan with the split end of a hickory stick.

"These woods are full of wild varmints," he began. "Dangerous ones like that bear today. We're going to have to take more care. Make sure to have our eyes open. And have a weapon at hand."

"Like the axe," said Will. "Or our knives."

Daniel nodded. "And above everything, like Pa says, never provoke a wild critter. Like with the fish."

Will stopped his scouring. "I couldn't let him have my fish," he protested. "Didn't we just have the tastiest meal since Pa left?"

"You could," Daniel said firmly. "You'll catch more. You've got to be more careful."

Will didn't say anything to that, just went back to scrubbing the pan, harder than before. His face had that set, stubborn look that meant it was no use talking anymore. If Pa was here, he'd likely talk sense into him with a good switching. But Daniel couldn't do that.

Maybe Will would be more careful and maybe he wouldn't. From now on, Daniel thought, he'd have to be more careful for both of them.

OCTOBER

7

Daniel woke up to a faint rustling sound. What could it be? he wondered. Some animal prowling around the cabin? He looked over at Will. His brother was still sleeping, and likely would go on sleeping even if a wild storm raged outside. Daniel rose silently and went over to the door, picking up the axe. Since their encounter with the bear, he always had the axe handy. Pushing aside an edge of the blanket, he peered outside.

At first he saw nothing in the early-morning light. No sign of any animal. Nothing out of the ordinary. He looked up into the trees.

A fair breeze had come up during the night. The wind rattled the branches, whipping them around and stirring the leaves, making them fall. Leaves were coming down in drifts, yellow and orange, red and brown.

The leaves, of course. That was the sound he'd heard. Daniel had noticed a colorful leaf here and there the past few days. On the path ahead when they walked down to fish. Floating on the water of the creek. On the vines wrapped tight around tree trunks, suddenly flashing red as fire. But now they were everywhere, tumbling out of the sky and skittering over the ground.

Fall was really here. Somehow Daniel had scarcely noticed the change. Mornings had been cooler, it was true. These days it took till midday for the sun to warm things up. And soon, he knew, the mornings would be downright cold. Daniel shivered in his thin tow shirt. Setting down the axe, he went to the fireplace to stir up the coals for breakfast.

When he had a good blaze going, he leaned over to count again the marks he'd scratched into the log. Twenty-five. No, twenty-six. He did a quick calculation in his head. Seven days to a week. Four weeks would be twenty-eight days. It was going on four weeks since Pa had left.

Why, Pa would likely be back with Ma and the family in just over a week's time. And he and Will hadn't even finished the chinking and daubing. Never mind the floor and chimney they'd thought to surprise Pa with. They had grown in the habit of stopping a little early in the afternoons to go down to the creek to fish. Will had gotten better and better with his fishing spear. And it was so good to have something to eat besides johnnycake.

But Daniel had made a promise to Pa to have the cabin ready. That meant at least to have the walls sealed up. And sticks cut for the chimney. And wood chopped and stacked for winter.

"Will!" he said. "Wake up."

Will's blanket stirred. His tousled head peered up from

his crumpled bed of leaves. He looked for all the world like their dog Trooper, Daniel thought.

"What?"

"Time's wasting," said Daniel. "We need to get to work."

They did no fishing that day. Will made trip after trip to the creek, but with the bucket, not his fishing spear. He lugged back the mud-clay and handed it up to Daniel, who stood on his log chair, stretching to reach the highest logs of the cabin wall.

As he sealed the cracks, the light in the cabin grew slowly dimmer. Of course, light still streamed in through the fireplace and the open door. But Daniel could imagine how dark it would be when both were closed. Yes, Ma would certainly want a window or two. Maybe Pa would even bring along a pane of window glass when he came.

The boys worked all afternoon, until it was too dark to see the cracks between logs. The dark came earlier now too, Daniel noticed. Especially in these woods, where the sun sank quickly behind the thick wall of trees like it was glad to go.

Neither of them gave a thought to fishing, they were that tired. They didn't even talk. Will cracked a few nuts, and they chewed on some leftover johnnycake. Daniel could barely stay awake while Will banked the fire. In minutes, they were both wrapped in their blankets, fast asleep.

47

It took three more days to finish the chinking and daubing. When the work was finally done, Daniel and Will walked around the inside of the cabin, looking it over.

"Looks pretty tight," said Will.

Daniel agreed. Here and there a little speck of light shone through where they'd missed a spot. Especially on the topmost logs, where he couldn't quite reach. They would have to be finished off when Pa came. But all in all, he thought, Pa would be satisfied. And Ma too. Not that this was the kind of home she was used to. She'd been raised near the great city of Philadelphia, where some of her kinfolk lived in houses made of clapboard and even brick. It was a start, though. It might take him a while, but Pa would make this cabin as comfortable as the farmhouse they'd left behind.

They moved right on to the woodpile. Daniel chopped and Will stacked, and when Daniel's shoulders began to ache, they traded places. They cut up fallen branches, some of the smaller logs lying around on the ground, and some small trees as well. Daniel set aside some of their branches in a separate pile, cutting them to size for finishing off the chimney.

After two days of chopping, the woodpile was so high, Will could barely lift the logs to place them on top.

"Isn't that enough?" he asked.

Daniel shook his head. Pa wouldn't think so. After all, who knew what kind of winter they would have out here in the wilderness? There might be months of icy cold and deep snow ahead. They had to make sure their fire would never go out.

"We'll start a new pile," he said.

All that chopping and stacking had made them hungry. Daniel thought he could eat just about anything, his stomach felt so hollow. So while Daniel was finishing the stacking, Will went off to the creek with his fishing spear.

"Watch out for bears!" Daniel called after him.

Will came back with two fair-sized fish. Though it wasn't yet supper time, Daniel dropped the log he was carrying and followed Will inside. They cooked up those fish right then and there.

"Ah," sighed Daniel, when he'd finished scraping out the smallest bits from the frying pan. "Those were some fine-tasting fish."

It was amazing how much better he felt. His stomach was like the fire in the fireplace, he thought. You had to keep feeding it, otherwise it wouldn't put out a blaze.

Now he felt ready to chop wood again.

"Come on, Will," he said. "Let's cut some more."

Finally, two days later, Daniel was satisfied that they had enough wood. Two piles, each half as high as the cabin, should take them a long way. And there were some good-sized logs in there, logs that would burn for a whole day or more.

Still, they weren't ready for Pa and Ma. Especially Ma. He wanted to make the cabin look welcoming to her when she came, so she wouldn't regret the move. She hadn't been eager from the start, moving so far away from her kinfolk. And on top of that, feeling so poorly all summer. Finding a half-built cabin deep in the forest with no human company for miles around could maybe even give her a turn for the worse.

He and Will rolled in two more log ends. They laid three short lengths of wood across them to make a low table. It was rough, but it made the cabin look a touch more civilized. On the table Daniel placed the cup he had finally finished carving. It too was rough, but it held water. And a bowl that Will had fashioned by burning out the center of a hard ash knot.

Then they swept the dirt floor with a broom made from the fine-split ends of a hickory branch. They carried out the old leaves and brought in new ones for beds. The just-fallen leaves smelled good and brought a touch of color to the cabin. Finally, they foraged for nuts, making a pile of them next to the meal sack so Ma would see a store pile of food when she walked in the door.

"Looks like the cabin is ready," Daniel said at last.

"Except for the fish," said Will, grinning.

"We'll wait till they get here for that," Daniel told him.

He counted the marks on the log, then counted them again to make sure. Thirty-five days. Exactly five weeks.

Pa and Ma could come today.

8

All afternoon they watched for Pa and Ma. And listened. Each small sound seemed like it could be Pa's shout or Zeke's high, excited voice calling their names. The boys stopped what they were doing and stood stock-still, waiting.

But no familiar figures stepped out of the trees. Disappointed, they turned back to their work.

Even that night, wrapped up against the cold on his new bed of leaves, Daniel thought he heard voices.

"What was that?" he whispered.

Will didn't answer. Of course, he was asleep.

It was only an owl, Daniel told himself. Pa wouldn't be traveling in the dark of night, not in this dense forest, not with the new baby. He knew that.

No reason why they would come on this particular day anyway. Pa had said five weeks, six at the outside. That could mean just about any day.

Best not to think about it. Best to keep busy.

So the next morning Daniel looked over the cabin again. More nuts, he thought. That was what they needed. Their little pile wouldn't last long once the whole family was here. Besides, nuts were plentiful now, and if they gathered a good amount, they could last well into winter. Ma would like that.

"Bring the bucket, Will," he said. "We're going to collect a real supply of nuts."

Thinking of the bear, Daniel picked up the axe. Then he set it down. It was too heavy to carry, and they wouldn't be going far from the cabin. Instead, he slipped his knife into his pocket.

They'd already gathered nuts along the path to the creek, so they struck off in the opposite direction. Daniel took care to notice where the sun was in the sky. That way there would be no trouble finding their way back.

Just as he'd thought, nuts were falling everywhere. Hickory nuts in their green shells. Light-colored walnuts. Bright brown chestnuts popping out of their spiny green jackets. The boys stooped to pick them up, dropping them into the bucket with a dull clatter.

Daniel kept a sharp eye out for bears, or any other wild critter that might have a liking for nuts.

"Look!" called Will. "A beech tree."

Beech nuts were sweet. Their little sisters, Sarah and Abby, would like them. Daniel followed Will to the base of a huge tree with sprawling limbs and pale gray bark. They dug under the carpet of leaves, coming up with handfuls of small, light-brown nuts.

Soon after that, Will spotted a butternut tree.

"Ma will want plenty of those," Daniel said. She used the green husks for dye when she made clothing for the family. Anything dipped into the dye pot turned a deep yellow-brown color that Ma specially favored.

It didn't take long to fill the bucket. Their pockets were bulging too.

"We best get back to the cabin," Daniel decided. "We can empty out the bucket and look for more."

He looked up at the sun to point their way home.

But there was no sun. The sky had clouded over. It was an even gray in every direction.

Daniel looked back over his shoulder. They'd come this way, hadn't they? Yes, they must have. Except that thick vine hanging down from that oak tree didn't look familiar. Nor did that mossy log sticking up at a broken angle.

"Will," he said. "Which way is the cabin?"

Will set down the bucket. "That way." He pointed in the other direction.

"Are you sure?"

Will turned around, studying the trees. "No," he admitted. "Could be the other way."

Daniel felt a flutter of fear rising in his stomach. He tried to swallow it down. They hadn't come that far from the cabin. They were bound to find their way back. Most likely the sun would come out again, and then he'd know. All he had to do was stay calm.

Looking up at the sky, though, Daniel knew the sun

wasn't coming back. It had grown darker, as if rain might be coming.

"We need to think on this," he said.

Slowly he walked around the butternut tree, searching for anything he might have seen before. Or any sign of their own tracks on the ground.

But leaves covered any tracks there might have been. And nothing else stood out to prod his memory. In the greenish light, all of those massive trees looked alike. They were a solid wall circling them on all sides. Daniel had the sudden strange feeling that the trees were saying something to him. *We are in charge here,* they whispered. *You are nothing compared to us. You cannot beat us with your puny axes and knives. We will do what we want with you.*

No, he couldn't think that way.

Daniel heard something. A small, skittering sound behind him. Turning, he saw a black squirrel run across the top of the broken, mossy log and disappear.

That must be the way they'd come. It had been his first thought, so most likely it was the right one.

"I say the cabin is this way," he told Will.

Will didn't argue. Picking up the bucket, he followed Daniel.

"Look for the trees where we gathered nuts," Daniel said.

That wasn't easy. There were so many trees, and the boys had been looking at the ground, not the trees, while they were collecting. He should have made a mark, Daniel thought. A blaze with his knife on a tree trunk every so often. That was what Pa would have done. But he had relied on the sun, and it had let him down.

It wouldn't matter, though, if he'd chosen the right way home. This was a lesson learned, and one he wouldn't forget.

Daniel scanned the trees up ahead. It seemed like they had walked far enough. Shouldn't they be seeing the opening where their cabin stood?

"I think it's that way," Will said suddenly.

He pointed off to the left. "I remember that chestnut tree! It's the one the bear was in."

Bounding ahead, Will circled the tree. "The path should be right here," he said. Then, shaking his head in disappointment, he muttered, "But it isn't."

They sat down to rest. The sky had grown darker still, Daniel noticed. Rain was definitely on the way. Soon they wouldn't be able to see where they were going.

"We better keep walking," he said. "Maybe we're almost there."

They trudged on. But no clearing opened up in front of them. No cabin, no path, no creek. Daniel could barely see where he was walking now. He tripped over a tree root and felt pain jolt his ankle. As he got slowly to his feet, the first raindrops touched his face.

They looked around for shelter.

"Over here!" cried Will.

A tree had fallen so its wide circle of roots was raised up, making a kind of slanting roof. The boys scrambled down into a hollow of leafy earth. It made a fair shelter, Daniel thought. They were protected for now from the rain, though if it kept up, water would seep down around them. For the moment, however, they were dry.

The rain did keep up, but more of a misty drizzle than a downpour. The trees above them dripped steadily. And darkness came.

"Looks like we have to stay here for the night," said Daniel.

They ate a few nuts for their supper, cracking them open with a heavy rock. They had a sharp taste, not as good as they'd be after they'd aged in their shells awhile. But Daniel was so hungry, he didn't care. Then he and Will smoothed out the leaves and soft earth underneath them. Without blankets, their root shelter felt cold and damp. That didn't seem to bother Will, though. He curled himself up just like old Trooper would, and soon was fast asleep.

Daniel wished sometimes he could take things as easily as Will. He lay awake, aware of the cold and of something hard under his backbone. He wondered if they were safe from wild critters. Could it be that they'd taken some animal's home? Would something come poking into their shelter while they slept? He'd better stay awake and on guard.

He took out his knife and laid it next to him. He listened for any sounds that might mean danger. But all he heard was the *drip, drip, drip* of rain in the trees. The sound was soothing.

Soon he too fell asleep.

Daniel awoke with a start. Something was wrong. He sat up, not sure for a moment where he was. Then he became aware that his shirt and britches were wet. Water was dripping next to him, turning the earth to mud. He shivered in the damp cold.

"Will!" he said.

Will was already stirring. "What happened?" he asked, sitting up.

"Rain came in while we were asleep. We best get out of here."

The rain had stopped and the sky was beginning to lighten as they crawled out of their shelter. Daniel was glad of that. But the morning air was cool. They had no fire to warm themselves or dry their wet clothes. The only way to warm up was to start walking again.

Looking at the trees half hidden by mist, Daniel had no better idea of which way to go than he'd had the day before. Might as well keep walking in the same direction, he thought, and hope to come on something they knew. And soon. He was so empty inside, it seemed like his stomach was about touching his backbone.

They ate more nuts, which helped a little, and began walking.

The sky brightened, but there was no sun. Not that it would have mattered. The sun couldn't point the way to the cabin now. Daniel had looked at so many gray-brown tree trunks, had climbed over so many mossy logs, and had pushed through so many brush thickets that he was hopelessly turned around in his head. He had the feeling they could be miles from the cabin or it could be just behind the next tree.

"Look there!" exclaimed Will.

Ahead was a butternut tree. Daniel blinked. That tree looked familiar. It couldn't be. But yes, at last they'd come on something they knew. The same butternut tree as yesterday.

They had walked in a circle.

All those hours of walking, and they had come out in the same place they'd started. What should they do now?

Daniel had no notion. He felt his eyes burn with tears. He couldn't think anymore, his head was spinning so. Like one of those little wooden tops Pa carved for Zeke. They were truly lost now. Seemed like any direction he thought to go would be the wrong one. It was no use going on, he thought. They would never find their way home.

His knees felt suddenly weak. He sank down under the butternut tree.

Will sat down next to him. Reaching into the bucket, he handed Daniel a chestnut.

"At least we know which way not to go," he said.

They sat and ate nuts, leaning against the rough, dark gray bark of the butternut tree. Slowly Daniel felt himself growing calmer. Think, he told himself. You have to think. What would Pa do?

Pa would figure things out. That's what he'd do. He

would study on a thing so long, you'd think he'd fallen asleep, and then, all at once, he'd come out with a plan.

Daniel stood up. He walked all around the butternut tree, looking and studying. Sure enough, after a few minutes a thought came to him. If they could find the creek, they could follow it to the cabin.

But how could they find the creek? He studied on that awhile till he had another thought. Water runs downhill. That was what Pa always said. So if they walked whichever way sloped down, they ought to find the creek. Only what if it turned out to be a different one? Daniel pushed that thought away. They had to try.

He walked around some more, looking. It seemed like every direction was pretty flat. Maybe, though, that way sloped down just a little. That was the way they'd go.

"Will," he said. "Listen. I have a plan."

Will didn't ask any questions. He seemed to be look-ing on Daniel now like he would Pa. That made Daniel feel good. It also made him hope hard that he was right.

How could they keep from walking in a circle again? Daniel needed to puzzle that out. This time the answer came quicker.

Looking off from the butternut tree, he lined up three more trees with his eyes. With Will following, he struck out for that third tree. He made a small cut in its bark with his knife. That would mark it in case they had to find their way back. He sighted three more trees in a line, and they moved on.

"Seems like we're going straight," he muttered to himself.

They tramped on so long, Daniel started worrying he'd picked the wrong way. It wasn't sloping down. There was no creek. He and Will were going to wander these unending woods till they were so tired and weak, they couldn't take another step. Then what would happen? Wolves? What was it Pa had said about wolves attacking the weak and wounded?

He wouldn't let that thought in.

Maybe he needed to study on this some more.

"Let's rest," Daniel said.

They sat on a hollow log and ate more nuts. That quieted the gnawing in his stomach, but Daniel couldn't help wishing they'd brought along some johnnycake. He thought of it covered with molasses. Or bee's honey, the way Ma served it up back home. He could see her table, covered with the pretty white cloth she'd woven herself, the one with roses in the corners. Set out with cool cups of milk and maybe some leftover chicken from last night's supper.

"Listen," said Will.

Did he hear something? Or was he just being wishful? Before Daniel could decide, Will was up and crashing through the bushes.

"It's here!" he shouted a moment later. "The creek!"

Daniel followed the sound. Down an incline, stumbling over roots and fallen branches, and then he caught sight of it. A silvery glitter between the trees, the wonderful, welcome sound of water.

"Hurrah!" he cried.

He slid the rest of the way down to the muddy bank. Dipping his hands into the cold water, he cupped them to drink. Daniel hadn't realized how thirsty he was. He drank and drank.

Will was leaning over the bank, splashing himself with water, ducking his whole face under to drink.

He grinned. "We found it! We're not lost anymore."

Was it true? Was this the right creek?

It looked right somehow, though it was flowing faster than he remembered, with more rocks and ripples. Daniel needed to stop again and study on it. Which direction would the cabin be? Upstream or down? He thought about it every which way, like he knew Pa would, looking at the water, the sky, the trees. Nothing came to him. Nothing but a feeling. The cabin was upstream.

Maybe sometimes, even for Pa, a feeling was all you had.

Daniel made a cut in a sapling tree near the water, in case he'd guessed wrong and they had to come back.

"Come on," he said to Will.

They followed the creek as near as they could, climbing over logs, sloshing through boggy places. Daniel didn't care now how wet he was. He no longer felt cold or tired or hungry. They were getting close, he thought.

He was first to see something he knew up ahead. That log half in, half out of the water. The patch of ferns near it. The place where Will had tried out his new fishing spear.

"Look!" he whooped.

Then they were running, tripping, and sliding along the bank until they caught sight of the path. Then racing along it, the half-full bucket of nuts bouncing against Will's knee. As they ran, Daniel had a sudden vision of Pa standing at the door of the cabin, Ma and the little ones waiting inside.

Oh, he'd be glad to see them. And glad too to let Pa be the one to figure things out once more.

He strained to see through the trees ahead.

There was no Pa standing by the door. Just the empty cabin with its half-built chimney, its blanket-covered door, the wood piled up on two sides, just the way they'd left it.

It didn't matter. Daniel was so glad to see the cabin, to be inside it again, to look on the axe in its place beside the door, the leaf beds with their blankets, the log chairs, the kettle and frying pan. And specially the sack of cornmeal next to the fireplace, ready to be cooked up into johnnycake to fill their empty bellies. It all looked so good to him.

"Oh." Will's face fell. "The fire's gone out."

Daniel looked at the ashes, gray and still in the fireplace. No need to touch them. They were surely cold.

The thing he'd vowed never to let happen had happened.

"We'll have to make a new one," he said.

It wasn't easy to start a new fire. Finally Daniel unraveled some threads from the ragged bottom of his shirt. Piling them on a piece of dry bark, he struck a spark with the flint Pa had left and his knife.

The spark fell onto the little nest of tinder. Daniel blew on it softly until, at last, he had a tiny flame. He and Will fed the flame with bits of dry leaves, then more bark. And finally they had a fire.

They were no longer lost, and they had a fire.

NOVEMBER

9

Six weeks at the outside. Daniel could hear Pa's words inside his head, clear as ever. But six weeks had passed. And now seven. Still there was no sign of Pa and Ma and the rest of the family.

What could have happened to them? Sickness maybe. Ma might still be feeling poorly. Or one of the little ones could have been taken sick. That would have kept them from starting out on time. Or it could be they had run into trouble on the way. Their wagon might have broken down in the mountains. Daniel had seen that happen on their own journey. As well as fierce storms that left huge fallen trees blocking the road. Or it might be they'd had trouble getting a boat to carry them upriver.

Any of those things could be the cause of the delay, he told himself. But Pa would keep going. He wouldn't let anything hold him back for long. Daniel had no doubt he'd be coming any day now.

In the meantime, though, he had new worries.

It was getting colder. Most of the leaves had fallen, leaving the trees stark and bare. Now the sun's rays could find their way through the treetops, yet they barely warmed the cabin. The days were growing shorter. The boys had to drag in larger logs to keep their fire burning all day. They were starting to use the woodpile.

Down at the creek, the water had turned icy cold, so cold that Will's feet grew numb as he stood holding his fishing spear. When he came out, he could barely stand. Soon, perhaps, the creek would freeze over. Then how would they catch fish?

Food was what worried Daniel most. The molasses jar was empty now, the salt just about gone, and the sack of cornmeal was going down surprisingly fast. They had plenty of nuts, but nuts weren't enough to fill their hungry stomachs. He had found that out when they were lost. If Pa didn't come soon, they could run out of food.

Clothing was another problem. He and Will had only their thin tow-cloth shirts and britches, which were becoming ragged. They had no wool coats for winter, no boots. And Will's shoes were about worn through, Daniel noticed when he left them on the creek bank to fish. Will never minded going barefoot, but he couldn't do that when winter came.

One more thing nagged at Daniel. It was a shadowy feeling, not clear in his mind but troubling just the same. Sometimes, coming out the cabin door in the morning or walking to the spring for fresh water, he had the odd sense that someone or something was watching him. It wasn't anything he could put his finger on. He never saw any sign of another human or a lurking wild animal, other than the squirrels and an occasional rabbit, which bounded away at his approach. Daniel tried to push it out of his mind. He was imagining things, he told himself. They had been alone too long. Still, he felt uneasy.

Waiting and worrying weren't going to help. He needed to do something. But what?

One morning, as he and Will were heading for the creek, they came on a rabbit sitting in the path just a few feet ahead of them.

Daniel reached out to grab Will's arm. They both stood still.

For a moment, no one seemed to breathe. Not the boys or the rabbit. Then Will's arm, holding his fishing spear, drew slowly back. The rabbit's long brown ear twitched.

Will hurled his spear. At the same instant, the rabbit hopped. The spear flew harmlessly into the brush. And in three more quick hops, the rabbit was gone.

"Not fast enough," Will muttered in disgust, picking up his spear. Luckily it was not broken.

The rabbit had been so close. Seeing it filled Daniel once more with a powerful longing for meat. Not like fish, which never quite filled you up, but something that stuck to your insides for a good long while. A rabbit stew! Oh, he could almost taste it.

Will must have been thinking the same thing. "I could make a heavier spear for hunting," he suggested as they continued down the path.

"Maybe," said Daniel.

He needed to think on this, figure it out. Would a heavier spear work? Or might it be better to try some kind of trap? Despite this accidental meeting today, it was hard to get close to a rabbit. Always its long ears and keen nose warned the animal that a human was near. Then it would bound off in quick, zigzagging hops, leaving you looking at its bouncing white tail. Will might hunt for hours and never get close enough to throw his spear. But a trap could be set and keep working while they did other things.

Yes, Daniel decided, a trap was the thing to try. How to make one, though, when they had no tools but an axe and a knife?

He studied on that all day. Something was nudging at the edges of his mind. Something Pa had said, maybe. He couldn't quite latch on to it, not until that evening when he sat with Will, starting to carve out another bowl by the light of the fire.

It came to him all at once. A while back, Pa had told him a story about his own pa when he was a young man. A bear had been troubling the settlement by stealing hogs, so he and his neighbors had gotten together and set a trap. And sure enough, they'd caught that bear and killed it. That was how Grandpap came to have a bearskin rug on the floor of his cabin.

Daniel had asked about the trap, he remembered. What kind of trap could catch a bear? And Pa had told him it was made of heavy logs, set so they would fall on the

70

bear when it came to take the bait. A deadfall trap, he called it.

That was all Daniel knew. But maybe they could build a trap almost like it, only smaller since they just wanted to catch a rabbit.

When he told Will, he seemed disappointed at first. Daniel knew he had his heart set on carving a new, heavier spear.

"Go ahead and make one," Daniel told him. "It will be good to have another weapon. But let's try setting a trap too."

The next day they began working on their rabbit trap. Just one log would be enough, Daniel figured, as long as it was a good, heavy one. He chose a log from the woodpile, and he and Will carried it to the spot where they'd seen the rabbit. They put it down a little way off the path, so it would look natural to a wild critter.

Now came the tricky part. They needed to raise one end and prop it up in such a way that it would come crashing down when the rabbit came to take the bait. It had to stay up till then, so the support had to be sturdy. But it had to fall easily when the animal brushed against it.

They tried different arrangements. A straight stick set on top of a rock. Or on top of two rocks. Or two sticks. Sometimes the log didn't fall. Sometimes it fell too easily.

"Owww!" yelped Will when it landed on his toes.

Finally Will came up with something Daniel would never have thought of. He whittled two sticks with his knife, and placed the point of one into a tiny groove in the middle of the other, then balanced that stick on a small rock. And it worked.

At least it seemed like it would.

"Now all we need is bait," said Daniel.

Grasses were what rabbits always seemed to be nibbling on. He and Will hunted around for anything green. Poking under fallen leaves, now dried and brown, they found a few bits of grass. Will wandered down to the creek and came back with a little more green stuff.

Daniel made a small pile of it. Carefully he placed the pile at the back of the trap, so the animal would have to walk all the way in to reach it.

"Looks tasty," said Will with a grin. "If I was a rabbit, I'd want to come in for a feed."

For a final touch, the boys drifted leaves around the edges of the trap so it looked like just an old, fallen-down log in the woods.

Daniel stood back, looking with satisfaction at their morning's work.

"You cannot catch *tschi mammus* like that."

Startled, Daniel whirled around. Behind him, tall and straight and dressed all in deerskins, was an Indian.

10

Daniel stood still, his legs frozen. His heart thumped loudly in his ears. All he could think of was there weren't supposed to be Indians left in these parts. Pa had said so.

What should he do? What should he say? Was the Indian alone, or were there more of them nearby? A war party? No, Pa had said the war between Indians and white men had been over for ten years now. Hadn't he?

"Why won't our trap catch a rabbit?" asked Will.

He was looking at the Indian with curiosity, but no fear. Will's mind was still on the trap, Daniel knew.

"Snare is better," said the Indian.

He spoke in a quick, quiet voice, the same way he moved. Because of this, Daniel had first thought he was young. But now he saw that the man's face was deeply lined and his black hair, long and pulled back from his face, was streaked with gray.

"I will show white boys," he said. And as suddenly as he had appeared, he faded noiselessly into the trees.

Daniel stared at the place where he had disappeared. Maybe his mind hadn't been playing tricks on him after all, he thought. Maybe this Indian had been watching them for days, even weeks. Why? What did he want with them?

"Will!" he whispered urgently. "Don't tell him about Pa being gone."

"Why not?" Will looked puzzled.

Why did Will always have to question everything? There was no time to explain.

"Just don't say anything," Daniel warned. "Let me do the talking."

A minute later the Indian reappeared. In one hand was a long, thin stalk of some kind of dry plant. It looked dead. What use could that be? Daniel wondered.

Swiftly the Indian peeled back the outside layer of the stalk. In a moment, he was twisting fine strands of fiber into a very thin rope. Then, before Daniel could understand how he'd done that, he was walking around in the brush, his eyes searching for something.

"Ah. Here is good spot," he said.

He picked up a straight stick and placed it across the low, forked branches of two saplings growing close together. Then he made a noose out of his plant rope and hung it from the stick so it reached almost to the ground.

"*Tschi mammus* comes by. Puts head in. Bam! Caught." The Indian smiled suddenly.

What was that strange word he used? It must be Indian for rabbit, Daniel decided.

"You make more snares," the man said. "Catch many *tschi mammus*."

He seemed friendly, Daniel thought. Still, he couldn't

let his guard down. Grandpap used to tell stories about the clever tricks Indians played on the white settlers back in the early days in Pennsylvania. They stole children and brought them up as part of their tribe. Sometimes the children weren't found until they were grown up. Or they never were found at all. This could be a trick.

The Indian was speaking again. "I am Solomon," he said.

That was a strange name for an Indian. A Bible name. Many was the night Ma had read to them the story of Solomon the wise man.

"White man gave me this name as a baby," the Indian explained. "At his mission."

"I'm Daniel." Daniel pointed at his brother. "He's Will."

Solomon nodded. Now what? How could Daniel find out what this Indian with the crazy name was doing here?

"You live in this cabin," Solomon said, jerking his head in the cabin's direction.

He *had* been watching them.

"No papa. No mama."

Of course, he knew that too. Daniel answered quickly, to make sure Will didn't. "Our pa went to fetch supplies." That much was true anyway. "He and Ma will be back any day now. Maybe today." He said it again, louder. "Most likely today."

Solomon nodded. "That is good," he said. "*Lo wan* will come soon. White boys need warm coats."

Lo wan, Daniel repeated to himself. Likely it meant winter. Or cold.

Will had been staring silently at the Indian for a long time. Daniel thought he was remembering his warning to keep quiet. But now, suddenly, he spoke.

"Do you live roundabout here?"

Solomon didn't answer for a long moment. His dark eyes gazed at the ground. When he lifted them, his face seemed clouded.

"Once upon a time, Lenape people lived here," he said. "Many, many years. Then white men came. There was much fighting. My father died. My brother died. Treaty says we must move. Some go north." He gestured again with his head. "My people go west. But I come back sometimes to trap skins."

Daniel felt something that had been strung tight inside him begin to loosen. Somehow he knew now that this Indian was not going to harm them. Along with a sadness in his eyes, there was kindness. Maybe Solomon would even help them.

That was what happened in the next few days.

Pa and Ma still did not come. But neither Solomon nor the boys spoke of that again. Nor did they speak about where the Indian had made his camp. Daniel thought it was somewhere upstream, but he didn't ask. He did ask Solomon how he came to speak English so well.

"I learn English as a boy at mission," he answered. "Some words I do not remember. But I speak with white men when I trade skins."

Almost every day Solomon would appear out of the trees, as suddenly and silently as he had the first day. Sometimes at the creek. Sometimes at the place he had set the snare, where the boys went each morning to check it and their trap. And once outside the cabin as Daniel was bringing in a load of firewood.

"Good," he said, nodding approvingly at the tall woodpiles. "Your fire burns all winter."

Daniel felt as pleased as he used to those rare times when Pa told him he'd done a good job.

Solomon was there the morning they found a rabbit tangled in the noose of his snare. It was still alive, though exhausted from struggling to free itself. Solomon broke off a heavy piece of branch and killed it with one blow.

"Dinner," he said, smiling. He held out the rabbit to Daniel by its ears.

Solomon would not join them in eating it, though Daniel and Will both asked. Maybe he knew just how hungry for meat the boys were. Or maybe he meant to keep his distance, Daniel wasn't sure.

"Fill your bellies," was all he said before disappearing again.

Daniel and Will filled their bellies with rabbit stew that night. Afterward, when they had scraped the pot clean, they lay back on their elbows a little way from the fire. Daniel was feeling warm and sleepy and full all the way to the top inside. He could barely remember the last time he'd felt that way.

"We need to learn how to set snares," Will said.

"Yes," agreed Daniel. "We'll ask Solomon tomorrow."

The next day they began asking questions.

Solomon showed them where to find the plant whose fiber he had used for his snare. He showed them how to twist the thin strings to make them stronger. "Use this for rope and for fishing net. For sewing shirts maybe," he said, looking at the boys' ragged clothing.

His quick flash of a smile made Daniel wonder if he was poking fun at them.

In an open place in the forest, where low bushes and high grasses grew, Solomon showed them how to set up snares on rabbit trails.

"Rabbits have trails?" Will said, surprised.

"Look close," said Solomon. "You see."

For the first time, Daniel and Will looked closely at the ground, at beaten-down grasses, barely bent stalks of plants, tiny broken-off twigs. At how wild critters lived.

"*Tschi mammus* is like man," Solomon told them. "He makes trail, from his house to water."

They set snares along these trails, concealed by leaves and brush. At first their snares were clumsy things, and Daniel thought the rabbits and other wild critters were probably laughing at them. But they learned quickly. Soon Will's clever fingers were twisting and tying almost as expertly as Solomon's. The third morning, when they went to check, they found a large rabbit dead in one of their snares, the noose tight around its neck.

Again the boys filled their bellies with rabbit stew.

Each day, it seemed, Solomon taught them something new. He showed them deer trails, though Daniel couldn't imagine how they could ever trap an animal as large as a deer. And an old Indian trail.

"If you follow half a day," Solomon said, "you come to a white man's mill."

That was good to know, Daniel thought. Their meal sack was dwindling fast. If Pa and Ma didn't come soon, they would surely run out.

On a cold, wet day, Solomon taught the boys a way to keep their feet dry. Gathering moss from the creek bank, he showed them how to stuff their shoes with it. Not only did the moss soak up the rainwater, but it kept Daniel's feet warm too.

Not Will's, though. His shoes were so worn out, the moss began seeping out the cracks as soon as he took a step. In a few more, it was gone.

"White boys' shoes are no good," Solomon said. "Moccasins better."

White boys. Why did he always call them that? Daniel thought he heard a touch of scorn in the words.

But Solomon helped Will tie his shoes together with rope made from twisted plant fiber.

What the Indian taught them most, though, was to see things. Really see them. To keep their eyes, and their ears, alert for danger, no matter what they were doing. And also to observe the smallest signs on the forest floor around them. Solomon had a stillness in him, whether he was sitting on the creek bank gazing into the water, or gliding noiselessly among the trees. Sometimes he would remain quiet a long time, not uttering a word, just staring at the ground. Then he would say something surprising.

"Wolves pass this way. Chasing deer."

He pointed at faint tracks in the damp earth, the rounded ones the wolves', the sharply pointed ones the deer's, far apart because they were running.

Or he would pick up a feather, so small and drab in color that Daniel never would have noticed it.

"Partridge nest is nearby."

Once, walking along the path near the creek, Solomon suddenly stopped.

"Look," he said.

Daniel and Will looked up. Sitting on a low branch, they made out the grayish-brown outline of a great horned owl.

Daniel took in a soft, whistling breath. It wasn't often you saw an owl in daylight. Especially a great horned owl. He'd seen one only once before, hunting in the woods back home with Pa.

"How did you know it was there?" asked Will. Solomon hadn't even looked up.

"Fresh droppings under tree."

Daniel would never have noticed. Whoever had given Solomon his name, he thought, had known he would grow into a wise man. And Daniel meant to remember his words for a long time. "Look close. You see."

The day after they saw the owl was the coldest they'd had yet. Winter was coming for sure. Daniel could feel it in his bones. A chill drizzle fell all day, and wind rattled the tree branches. Daniel and Will kept inside, except for a quick trip out by Will to check their snares.

He came back empty-handed. "Our deadfall trap fell down," he reported. "Nothing inside. Solomon was right, snares are much better."

Solomon didn't appear that day. Nor the next. Daniel didn't think much of it, as the Indian always came and went without saying a word, and some days didn't come at all. Tending to his traps, Daniel figured.

But by the third day, he began to wonder. Could Solomon have gone away, back to his people in the west, without saying good-bye? Daniel didn't think he would do that. Might something have happened to him? An accident perhaps? Daniel couldn't help remembering with a shiver their encounter with the bear. It could be Solomon needed their help. But they didn't even know where to look for him.

More than likely, Daniel told himself, he was just busy with his traps.

On the morning of the fourth day, Daniel was at the woodpile when he felt that old feeling of someone watching him. He turned around, his arms full of wood, and there was Solomon.

He knew before the Indian spoke that he had come to say good-bye. He carried a pack on his back, so heavily loaded with skins that he seemed bent under their weight. His face was solemn, its lines deeper than usual.

"I must go now," he said, jerking his head toward the west. "I come to say good-bye."

Will stepped out of the cabin.

"Will you come back?" he asked.

"Sometime maybe," Solomon answered. He took something from his pack and held it out to Will. "A present."

Daniel stared. In Solomon's hand was a pair of buckskin moccasins just like the ones he wore himself.

"White boy needs *wusk baxen* for winter. I made them for you."

Will was staring too. Then he grinned and gave a loud whoop. "Moccasins! Real moccasins. Hurrah!"

Daniel remembered his manners. What would Ma say if she was here?

"We thank you kindly, Solomon," he said.

Solomon nodded. "Papa and Mama come soon."

Was it a question? Daniel wasn't sure. But he nodded back.

"Very soon," he said. "Maybe today."

"Good," said Solomon.

With a slight wave of his hand, he turned and walked into the trees.

DECEMBER

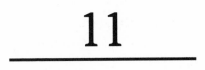

11

Daniel felt strange when he woke the next morning. What was it? What was different? For a moment, he couldn't remember. Then he did. Solomon. He was gone, and they were alone again.

He was alone. Will was a help, no doubt about it. He could do things Daniel wasn't good at, like figuring how to catch fish with a spear and fashioning rabbit snares so easily with his hands. He was willing to do most anything, and cheerful about it too. But when it came to what Ma called common sense—thinking things through before jumping into them—Daniel was the one who had to take charge.

Pa should be the one taking charge. Where are you, Pa? he asked silently, looking up at the cabin roof. Little slits of daylight shone through. That was where the water would come dripping in when heavy snows came. As they would. And soon, most likely. Daniel had no doubt Pa could fix the roof. But he himself had no thought of how to do it.

What could have happened to Pa and Ma? Daniel felt a sudden sharp pang deep in the pit of his stomach. For so long, he'd gone on thinking they would get here any day now. If not today, then tomorrow. Only the days kept going by. His knife marks now covered almost the whole bottom log next to the fireplace. Last time he'd counted, they added up to close to eighty. That was ten weeks. No, eleven. Something real bad must have happened. That was the only way Pa could not be here. Daniel didn't want to think of what that something could be.

It's useless to lie abed thinking this way, he told himself. Better to be up and doing. Getting ready for the winter that was coming whether Pa and Ma got here or not.

"Will!"

Daniel rousted his brother out of bed.

"It's c-c-cold," Will grumbled as he struggled to his feet.

They both stay wrapped in their blankets, shivering, until Will got the fire built up again. Breakfast of hot cornmeal mush quieted Daniel's shivers and warmed his insides. That reminded him. As soon as they finished eating, he set about figuring how much meal they had left.

Only a few precious grains of salt remained at the bottom of the salt sack. Carefully, he shook them out. Then Will held the sack open, while Daniel began transferring the meal by cupfuls from the larger sack to the smaller one, counting as he went.

"How much is there?" Will asked. For once, he seemed anxious. More than likely, he hadn't given a thought till now to the meal sack going down.

Daniel calculated a moment.

"Enough to last about two weeks, I expect," he said. "Maybe three, if we're careful."

Two or three weeks wasn't long. Especially in winter. What if a heavy snow were to trap them inside the cabin?

It was plain that they couldn't wait many more days for Pa and Ma. Daniel was going to have to take that Indian trail Solomon had showed them to the mill.

Before he made such a journey, though, he needed warmer clothing. What could he do about that?

Looking around the cabin, Daniel's eye fell on his bed of leaves. His blanket! Of course. Besides the fire, the blankets were their only source of warmth. If he cut up one of them, he could fashion a rough coat for himself, and most likely one for Will as well.

Should he use his blanket? Or the one that Pa had hung over the doorway till he could make a proper door?

If he used his own, then he and Will would have to share a blanket for sleeping. But if he used the one covering the doorway, there would be nothing between them and the wild critters outside. Having a door covering was a comfort somehow, even though he knew it wouldn't keep out anything that really wanted to come in. Daniel decided to use his own blanket.

"We're going to make ourselves some winter coats," he told Will.

They set to work.

The first thing Daniel did was spread his blanket out

flat on the dirt floor. He had Will lie down at one end. Using his knife, sawing away at the surprisingly tough strands of wool, he slowly cut out the shape of a coat. He used this as a pattern to cut out a second piece just like it. This would be Will's coat.

Then they switched places, and Will cut out a coat for Daniel. The blanket was just big enough, with some scraps left over for patches if something, like their britches, gave out later on.

Next came the hard part, sewing the two halves of the coats together. As long as Daniel could remember, he had seen Ma sitting in her rocking chair next to the fire in the evenings, sewing new clothes or stitching up rips in old ones. But he had never paid any attention to how she did it. All he could call to mind was her needle darting in and out, flashing brightly in the firelight.

They had no needle or any kind of thread. No, that wasn't so. What was it Solomon had said? The plant fiber they had used for snares could be used for sewing too.

Daniel sent Will out to find more of it.

"Bring back as much as you can," he said. It was sure to have other uses as well in the coming winter.

While Will was gone, Daniel tried to shape a needle out of a long sliver of wood. It kept breaking just when he got it small enough. Maybe, he thought, he ought to try a tiny piece of bone. That was what the Indians used. In the end, though, he decided they didn't need a needle. He poked holes with the point of his knife along the edges of the coat pieces, and he and Will wound the plant-fiber thread through them.

The work took most of the day to finish, and there was no question of buttons or any of Ma's other finishing touches. But at last they both pulled their blanket coats over their heads.

"It's warm!" Will exclaimed happily.

"It fits," said Daniel, relieved.

The coats were long, coming all the way down to cover their knees. That was a good thing, Daniel figured, since their britches were so thin.

They went outside to try them out.

The day was cloudy, with a cold wind blowing. A wintry wind.

"I'm warm as a tick in a bearskin!" Will said, grinning. He did a little dance in his new coat and moccasins, flinging out his feet and prancing in a circle by the cabin door.

Daniel felt warm too in his blanket coat. Warmer than he had for weeks. And just in time.

Because something was in the air. A cold dampness. A certain look to the low, gray sky. And a smell. Daniel remembered that smell from other winters. From Pa sniffing the air as they walked back together from feeding the animals in the barn.

Snow. Snow was on the way.

12

It didn't snow that night. Instead, rain and sleet ticked against the cabin roof all night long. Daniel heard it, huddled against Will's back under their one blanket. And when he looked out the door the next morning, he saw it on the branches of the trees. A thin, shiny glaze of ice.

The sun came out by mid-morning, melting the ice, sending chunks of it down to shatter on the roof. Daniel worried one of them would go right through. But Pa had done a good job laying down the sheets of bark. The roof held.

That decided him somehow. Tomorrow, before another storm came, he was going to walk to the mill.

When he told Will, his brother's face lit up.

"I'm going too," he said happily. "I'll take my new spear. It's just about finished. Maybe I can hunt some game on the way."

Daniel looked at him.

"No," he said. "You stay here."

Will's face darkened.

"Pa would let me go," he argued, his chin lifting stubbornly. "It's not right to have to stay behind, just because I'm younger."

"It's not that," Daniel said quickly. "One of us needs to be here if Pa and Ma come. If they saw an empty cabin, what would they think? Besides, we need to set out more snares. With winter coming on, game may get scarce. You can do that while I'm gone."

Will glared at him, his mouth set in a straight line, but he didn't say anything more.

Just before sunup the next morning, Daniel made a little bundle of johnnycake and some nuts for the journey. Then, wearing his blanket coat, the empty meal sack slung over his shoulder, he set out.

He felt a little pang of doubt as he walked away from the cabin. Maybe he should have let Will come too. What if he got lost? Or met a bear, or wolves? Wouldn't he and Will be better off staying together?

But one of them ought to be at the cabin if Pa and Ma came.

If. They hadn't come all these past days, these past weeks. Why would they come today?

Daniel realized that he had another reason for going alone that he hadn't told Will. He had set a kind of test for himself, going on this journey without Pa, without Solomon, without Will. Without all those who weren't afraid of anything.

He found the Indian trail Solomon had showed them easily enough. Daniel worried that he'd have trouble following it, but he took care to use his eyes as the Indian had shown them. "Look close. You see." The trail

91

appeared to have been beaten down by years of travel by horses' hooves and human feet. For a good while it followed close to the creek, then branched off. Up rises and down into hollows. Then back along the creek again. He kept an eye on the sun so this time he'd know which direction he was going. South, he decided. Mostly south. And to make sure he didn't get lost on the way back, he cut blazes into trees wherever the trail became indistinct.

His blanket coat was just right. It kept him warm, in fact almost too warm as the sun rose higher in the sky. When he judged he'd been walking about two hours, Daniel sat down for a rest and a bite of johnnycake.

Leaning back against the broad trunk of a chestnut tree, chewing on his johnnycake, he felt good. He was on his way to the mill to fetch meal for the winter. Could be he'd get to talk to another settler or two living here-abouts. He was having no trouble following the Indian trail. Except for an occasional squirrel scuttling about overhead, he hadn't seen any sign of wild varmints. The day was fine, and he was warm inside his blanket coat.

Then, in an instant, everything changed. Daniel heard a noise behind him. A kind of shuffling in the leaves. And behind him on the other side, hidden by the tree trunk, another small sound. Some creature was creeping up on him. More than one, by the sound.

Wolves? Daniel grasped his knife. But what good would it do against a pack of wolves? He'd be better off climbing a tree. Not this one, though. Its trunk was too massive, its branches too high to reach.

He looked around frantically for a smaller tree—just as the creatures came into sight.

Turkeys! Six or seven wild turkeys. Their oval bodies were so dark, they blended into the low brush. Their long necks and small, bluish-colored heads were bent to the ground, looking for food.

Daniel didn't know who was more surprised, he or the turkeys.

"Pit-put! Pit-put!" they squawked.

The birds flapped their wings, making them look suddenly fat. And then they were gone. Running quickly for such awkward-looking creatures, they disappeared into the trees.

Daniel had to smile. The turkeys had looked so shocked to come upon him, and so funny running away. A minute later he felt that old uneasiness creeping over him again, knotting his insides. You never knew what you would encounter in these woods, that was the thing. You never knew what might lurk among these dark, looming, unfriendly trees.

Daniel didn't linger any longer. He walked quickly, his eyes alert, his hand ready to reach for his knife. He didn't stop again until the sun was high in the sky. Coming around a bend in the creek, which by now had dwindled to a small trickle of a stream, Daniel saw what appeared to be a shed.

It was roughly built, two stories high, but open below. In the open part, two horses were walking in a circle.

What was this? Not the mill Daniel had expected. Not the kind he knew back home in Pennsylvania. There a mill was a sturdy building, likely built of stone, with a large turning wheel on the outside, situated on swiftly-moving water.

As he came closer, he saw that the horses were pushing against long poles that were turning something. A good-sized post, it looked like, that ran up into the second story. Then he remembered that Grandpap had talked one time about mills powered by horses.

A man stepped out of the shed. He was bulky, dressed in layers of torn and dirty clothing, his bearded face shaded by a wide-brimmed hat. He pushed back the hat, staring at Daniel.

"Howdy there, boy," he greeted him.

His face was friendly enough, Daniel thought.

"Howdy," he said, setting down his meal sack.

"Name's Tom Cochran," the man went on, thrusting out his hand. "This here's my horse mill."

Daniel's hand was nearly crushed in his grip. "I'm Daniel Griffith," he said.

The man nodded. "Heard tell you folks was settling around here. Where's your pa today?"

"He's gone to Pennsylvania to fetch my ma and the rest of the family. He'll be back any day now," Daniel answered. He sounded just like he had when he talked to

Solomon, he thought. Wishfully thinking. "I was wondering if I could get some meal."

"You got some corn to grind?" Tom Cochran looked around as if he expected Daniel had hidden it somewhere.

"No, sir. I'd need it on account. My pa will pay you when he gets here. It's just me and my brother have about run out."

The miller looked him up and down. Then he shrugged his large shoulders. "Guess I can do that," he agreed. "Only you'll have to wait. I got those two boys ahead of you."

He motioned at two men Daniel hadn't noticed before. They were around the side of the shed, one leaning against it, the other standing with what looked like a small axe in his hand. As Daniel watched, the man reared back and threw the axe at a slim sapling tree. It split the wood right down the middle, and both men laughed loudly.

"Might as well set down and make yourself comfortable," Tom Cochran said, walking back into the shed.

Daniel heard wood creaking and grinding stones rumbling inside as the mill turned. He meandered over to where the two men were standing.

"Howdy," he said.

The young man with the axe was Jake Hutchins and the other was his brother Sam. They were both scrawny thin, like whips of sapling trees. The two of them lived over by Wolf Creek, Jake told him. Daniel wasn't sure where that was, but from the direction Jake pointed, he could tell it wasn't close to their cabin.

Jake was the talkative one, helped out by a bottle he and Sam kept passing back and forth.

"See this here tomahawk?" he said, turning the axe over in his hands. "Our pa got it off an Indian he killed back in '93. Yep, our pa and his brothers killed them a pack of redskins. Drove those varmints out of the country pretty much all by themselves."

Daniel thought of Solomon and his sad eyes. Solomon wasn't a varmint, he thought indignantly. But he didn't say anything. Better just to keep quiet and listen.

Jake was full of stories. First about the horse mill. Daniel sat and cracked nuts while Jake talked.

"Used to be," he began, "a man named Logan had himself a water mill here. But then the dry years came along and this here creek shrunk up to nothing. So old Logan shut down. Couple of years back, Tom Cochran got the idea of running the mill by horse power. Takes longer, and you got to supply your own horses. But it does the job. Better than going all the way to Willow Springs."

That story sounded true enough. But Daniel wasn't so sure about some of his other tales.

"I expect you've heard of Dayton Riley, haven't you, boy?"

Daniel shook his head.

96

"Well, Dayton Riley was the greatest hunter in all of Northwest Territory. He lived right near here in a great big sycamore tree. That's right, made himself a home inside a hollow old tree. He dressed all in buckskins and had a beard that came down halfway to his toes. He was quite a sight, I can tell you. He'd hunt anything that moved, but bears was his particular favorite. Claimed to have shot over five hundred of 'em. Ma always said stay away from Dayton Riley, he's crazy as a coot, but me and Sam talked to him once, didn't we, Sam?"

Sam nodded. "Gave us the skin of a bear cub and Ma made it into winter hats."

That led to another story.

"Speaking of crazy as a coot," said Jake, "puts me in mind of Mad Mary. She was an Indian fighter. After her husband was killed in the French War, she went on the warpath against them all by herself. She dressed like a man, shot like a man, drank whiskey and chewed tobacco like a man, and rode a big black horse. The Indians never could catch her, and after a while got to be afraid of her. They were the ones gave her the name Mad Mary."

"What happened to her?" Daniel asked.

"She lived to a ripe old age. Built herself a little cabin made of fence rails, I hear tell, and lived there like a wild animal. Had no furnishings, not even a bed. Once in a while she'd paddle her canoe to the nearest town, gun slung over her shoulder, and scare all the young folks."

Sam took another swig from the bottle. "Yep," he said,

grinning. "Them was the days. Before this country started getting all settled up."

"All settled up?" Daniel couldn't help being surprised. These woods were empty as far as he could tell.

Jake nodded. "Folks is coming in from everywhere—Kentucky, Carolina, Tennessee. Why, we got a neighbor not ten miles from our place. Even hear talk of building a school."

Ma would be glad to hear that, Daniel thought. It was one of her worries about moving out here that they'd all grow up ignorant. Truth to tell, he'd be glad of it too. He missed the books the schoolmaster, Mr. James, used to lend him back home. Books like *Morse's Geography* and *Pilgrim's Progress*. The only book Pa and Ma had was the Bible.

"If it comes to that," said Sam, shaking his head, "we're moving on. Farther west, where there's room to breathe."

It was strange, Daniel thought, that something could look one way to one person and just the opposite to another. Well, as Ma would say, that's what makes the world go round.

Tom Cochran came around the side of the shed.

"You two are all set," he said. "Unless you want to lend this boy the use of your horses for his meal."

" 'Course we can," Jake agreed. He and Sam didn't seem in any hurry to leave. Now they were chewing on some dried meat jerky.

"I surely do thank you," said Daniel.

A few stories and swigs from the bottle later, Jake and Sam loaded their meal sacks onto their horses. Daniel lifted his half-filled sack onto his shoulder. It was heavy. He could have used Will's help in carrying it. Still, he was glad he had come alone.

"My pa will be over to pay you," he told Tom Cochran.

Waving good-bye to Jake and Sam, he set off for home.

As he rounded the bend in the creek, Daniel noticed that the sun was starting to sink down behind the trees. He'd stayed longer than he planned, what with the slow grinding of the horse mill and all Jake's stories. It had been good to hear voices other than his own and Will's, to know they weren't quite alone out here. But he should have been paying attention, he told himself. Now he'd have to hurry to get back to the cabin before dark.

And there was the meal sack. It was heavier than he'd expected. He would have to stop and rest now and again on his way.

It was a good thing he'd marked the trail with his knife. With those blazed trees to follow, at least he didn't have to worry about getting lost.

Daniel hurried along as fast as he could. Along the slowly widening creek. Turn north up that small rise. Keep an eye out for a blazed tree. Yes, there it was. Every now and then he looked up at the sun. *Don't you go down yet,* he told it. *Stay a little longer.*

He had to stop to rest several times, but he didn't rest long. Just took a bite of johnnycake or a quick drink from the creek, shifted the meal sack to the other shoulder, and kept walking.

The sun kept sliding down. Lower and lower. And then, in a blink, it was gone. All that was left was a faint glow in the west.

He didn't have much farther to go, Daniel told himself. He could still see the trail. And the fresh cuts he'd made stood out against the dark trunks of the trees. He'd be all right.

Slowly everything turned to gray. Light gray, darker gray, then black.

That was when he began to hear things. Tiny rustlings. The smallest movement in a tree above his head. Was anything there, or was he just getting spooked by the coming darkness?

A minute later he was sure something was following him. Something on quiet, padding feet. He could hear it plainly behind him. Or maybe more than one. Wolves? Could it be wolves?

Daniel turned around quickly. And caught a glimpse of a doglike dark shadow melting into the trees.

A wolf for sure. And mostly likely more. Maybe a whole pack of them. His heart pounding, Daniel struggled to think. What should you do if wolves were following you? Had Pa ever said anything about it, or Grandpap? He couldn't remember. All he could think of was what Pa had said that time about wolves going after the weak and wounded.

Just keep walking, he decided. Don't let them think you're weak or scared.

He glanced over his shoulder again. This time he saw nothing but the long black legs of trees. Oh, why had he waited so long to start back? How had he allowed himself to be walking through the woods in darkness?

Now the trees seemed to be answering him. *Foolish,* they said. *Foolish, foolish, foolish.*

He was nearly to the cabin, Daniel thought. It had to be just around the next bend. He kept walking, feeling the heavy weight of the meal sack on his aching shoulder. Don't look back, he told himself. Just keep going.

Footsteps padded behind him. They seemed to be coming closer.

Daniel stumbled on. All at once he saw it. A dark, squarish shape right ahead. Tall stacks of wood on either side. Someone moving next to the open door.

"Will!"

Somehow he found the strength to run forward as his brother came to meet him.

"You're back!"

Even in the dim light, Daniel could make out the relief on Will's face.

He set down the sack at last by the cabin door.

"I got the meal," he said.

JANUARY

13

The first snow came two days later. Large flakes danced in the air, swirling white against the dark trees, then melting quickly as they touched the ground. The snow seemed to stop as darkness fell. But when Daniel looked out the door the next morning, the branches of the trees were etched in white. A light coating covered the stumps and the woodpiles. He brushed it off as he carried in more firewood.

Better bring in extra, he thought. Keep a good-sized pile next to the fireplace in case the next snow is deep. And get a good supply of water too.

His hands were cold. If he were home, he'd be wearing the heavy gray mittens Ma knitted for all of them, made from the wool of their own sheep. What could he do for mittens here?

He and Will talked about it while they ate their breakfast of hot mush. Will had cooked up a bigger pot this time, Daniel noticed. Since his trip to the mill, it was a relief not to have to skimp on meal.

"We could use the scraps from our blanket coats to make mittens," Daniel suggested.

That would likely do for most days. Still, if it got really

cold, one layer of wool wouldn't be enough to keep their hands warm. How did wild critters stay warm on the coldest days?

"Or maybe rabbit skins," said Will.

That was it. Animals had their fur to keep them warm. Why hadn't he thought before of saving the skins from the rabbits they'd caught? Daniel was beginning to see that you couldn't waste anything living in these woods. That was one of the lessons Solomon had been trying to teach them, only he hadn't been paying close enough attention.

"That's what we'll do," Daniel decided. "We'll make rabbit fur mittens."

It took a few days to catch the rabbits they needed. Two or three would be enough, Daniel figured. This time the boys were as interested in the skins as the meat. Carefully, they slit them from top to bottom. They scraped the skins clean, then worked them with their hands to keep them soft. Feeling the fur against his fingers, Daniel could tell these mittens would be plenty warm. Warmer even than Ma's.

As with their blanket coats, they used themselves as patterns, cutting around their hands to make mitten shapes. Again, they poked holes along the edges with a knife point and used fiber thread to sew the two halves together, the fur on the inside.

Will tried his on. "They're warm," he said, "but sort of stiff."

106

Daniel agreed. The rabbit fur would keep them warm on the coldest of days. And though the skins were stiff now, most likely they would soften up with use.

"Maybe we could make hats too," suggested Will.

Of course. They would collect more rabbit skins and fashion them into warm fur hats. Perhaps, Daniel thought, they could even use rabbit fur to line their shoes.

He had only one worry. What would happen when the deeper snows came? Would they still be able to catch rabbits in their snares? Or would the rabbits, along with other small creatures, sleep through the coldest days of winter in warm burrows? And what about fish? If the creek froze, as it was likely to, would the fish still be there under the ice? Could Will break through and spear them? Now that they had enough meal, would they have anything else to eat in the weeks ahead?

The next few days were wintry cold and damp. A slow drizzle fell off and on, mixing with brief flurries of snow. The trees seemed to hunch over them, looming dark and heavy against the gray sky. It was as if they were bracing themselves, Daniel thought, for harsh weather to come.

Each morning the boys checked their snares. One day they had a rabbit, and they saved its skin for their fur hats. Another day they found a possum. Daniel didn't favor the taste, but it would make a change from rabbit. For several days after that, though, they found nothing in their traps. Once again, Daniel wondered if winter weather was making game scarce.

One morning they woke to find a new dusting of snow on the woodpiles. The air was so cold, Daniel's ears felt nipped with frost as he and Will walked down to the creek. Just as he'd feared, Daniel saw that a thin coating of ice had formed across the widest part, where the water moved most slowly.

Will broke a hole in the ice with the heavy end of his fishing spear. He peered into the dark water.

"Can't see much," he muttered, frowning.

He couldn't stand in the water now that it was so cold. How would he be able to spear fish?

Will tried fishing from the creek bank, but that didn't work. Nor did standing on a rock in shallow water. He thrust his spear at a small ripple, and nearly slid into the stream himself.

But Will didn't give up. He never would. Back home, he'd try anything that anyone said couldn't be done. Swimming across a pond, shooting a squirrel out of a tall pine tree, jumping off a rock ledge. He'd hurt his foot so bad that time, Ma thought it was broken.

Will stepped onto the old rotting log that lay half in, half out of the water.

"Be careful," warned Daniel. "It's slippery."

Will walked slowly to the end, where the log began to submerge into the creek. He turned around, grinning.

"My moccasins don't slip at all," he said. "Much better than those old shoes."

He cracked the ice all around the log with his spear. Crouching down, he stared for a long time into the water. Daniel was surprised all over again at how patient Will could be. Just as he had so many times before, he waited without moving for a fish to come by.

It was a long wait. Daniel's feet got so cold, he could barely feel his toes. He stamped on the wet, hard bank to get his blood moving. He was beginning to think the fish were all sleeping in the frozen mud, when suddenly he saw Will's spear dart into the water.

Excitedly Will lifted it out. "I got—" he started to say, then looked down in dismay. "Oh. It got away."

"But you saw it?" Daniel asked anxiously. "You saw a fish?"

Will nodded. "They're down there. And I'm going to catch one."

Stubbornly he stayed on the log, his spear ready in his hand. He'd stay there till their feet froze into solid blocks of ice, Daniel thought. Pa wouldn't let that happen if he was here. He'd tell Will not to be foolish, he had to quit now. Come back and try again another day.

Daniel was just forming those words, when Will gave a sudden yelp.

"Ahhh!"

He looked up to see the fishing spear stuck straight up in the water, and Will struggling to keep his balance on the end of the log. His arms waved crazily in the air, then one foot slipped out from under him. With a loud splash, he fell into the creek.

Daniel's first thought was to rush in and pull him out. But Will was already on his feet, in water that barely covered his knees. He was holding up his spear in triumph. On the end of it was a large, wriggling fish.

"Got him!" he crowed happily. "My biggest one yet!"

He was grinning from ear to ear as he waded to shore. Luckily he hadn't lost his moccasins. And he hadn't been wearing his rabbit fur mittens. His britches and blanket coat were sopping wet, though, and covered with mucky leaves and twigs. Even his hair was plastered with mud. He stood dripping on the bank.

"It's c-cold," Will mumbled, suddenly shivering.

Daniel saw that his face was gray. As gray as fireplace ashes. And now his whole body was shaking.

"Come on," he said. "We need to get to the cabin."

"F-f-f-i-i-sh." Will could barely get out the word, but Daniel knew. He wasn't going without his fish.

"I've got it," he said.

His arm around Will's shoulders, Daniel hurried him up the path. Will couldn't speak at all, just kept shaking all over like someone with the palsy. Now his face was turning blue.

Inside, Daniel piled wood onto the fire until it blazed up bright and hot. Then he stripped off Will's wet clothes. He wrapped him in their bed blanket and sat him as close as he could to the fire. But Will couldn't stop shaking. Daniel took off his own coat and wrapped that around him too. Will looked up at him gratefully. Still, he kept shivering.

What else could he do? Daniel tried to think. If Ma was here, she would make Will a steaming cup of tea with her special brew of herbs. "Drink this," she'd say, "before you catch your death of cold." Daniel couldn't do that. All he could think of was to cook up some hot mush.

He made a batch, keeping one eye on Will all the while, and fed small bites of it to him. After that, he cleaned the fish and roasted it over the fire. By then, Will's color was starting to return. But he still had bouts of violent shivering.

"M-mighty tasty f-f-ish," he croaked, trying to grin.

"Shhh," said Daniel. "Don't talk."

Why hadn't he stopped Will before he fell into the creek? Daniel thought. He should have known something like this would happen. What if Will really did catch his death of cold?

They sat quietly close to the fire. Whenever the flames began to die down, Daniel piled on another large log. He was going to keep the cabin warm no matter how much wood it took. No matter if he had to stay awake all night to do it.

Finally he noticed that Will had fallen asleep. He watched his brother's thin chest moving slowly, evenly, up and down. Good, it looked like the shaking had stopped at last. Daniel let out a long breath of relief. More than likely, Will would be all right in the morning.

Daniel kept watching him, just to make sure. After a while his eyes wandered over to the big log next to the fireplace, to all the marks he'd made with his knife, counting the days till Pa's return. He hadn't made any marks the last few days. He'd been so busy or so tired at night, he'd forgotten to do it. Or maybe there was another reason. Maybe he was no longer expecting Pa and Ma and the rest of the family to arrive at the cabin any day now.

Daniel didn't know anymore how many weeks it had been. He couldn't think about why they hadn't come or if they ever would.

All he knew was it was winter now. And he and Will were on their own.

14

It started with a few thin flakes falling slowly out of a pewter-gray sky. Daniel thought they would stop, as they had so many times before. But the snow continued to fall. It came down all morning, as the boys checked their snares and carried in wood for the fire. And all afternoon, as they skinned the good-sized rabbit they'd caught and began preparing the skin to become part of a rabbit fur hat. As the sky darkened into night, Daniel looked out the cabin door. The snow was coming down fast now, a thick swirling curtain of white that hid everything behind it.

Daniel woke several times in the night, listening—he wasn't sure for what. He heard no sounds outside. No chorus of wolves or low hooting of owls this night. All was silent.

And silence was all he heard when he awoke the next morning. As he slipped out from under the blanket, leaving Will still sleeping, his hand brushed against something cold and wet. Snow! A powdery coating of white covered their blanket. Looking around, Daniel saw little piles of snow here and there along the cabin walls. It must have drifted in through cracks in the logs where the chinking wasn't tight or had begun to fall out.

He hadn't done as good a job on the chinking as Pa would have, Daniel thought with a pang. He and Will had hurried, and taken time out to go fishing. Pa would have gone over those log walls until you couldn't see a peep of daylight anywhere. And he'd have been watching to see if any of the chinking fell out, and replacing it if it did.

Well, nothing could be done about that now. It would have to wait till warmer weather, when they could dig more clay. Daniel stirred up the fire and piled on two new logs, then went to the door to look out.

As he pulled aside the blanket, snow fell in on his feet. Snow was piled up all around the cabin. It covered the two woodpiles so he could barely make out where they were. Snow clung to the sides of the dark tree trunks. It had buried the stumps, which looked like low, round, white hills. Daniel couldn't tell how much had fallen. But he guessed if he stepped out into it, he'd be up to his knees at least.

"What happened?" asked Will behind him, rubbing sleepy eyes. He had snow in his hair, Daniel noticed.

"Snowed all night," Daniel said. "And it's still snowing."

It snowed all that day too. Each time Daniel looked out the door, he saw the flakes falling steadily, piling higher and higher around the cabin. In the afternoon a cold wind came up, blowing the snow around. More of it sifted in through the openings between logs and around the blanket door.

At dusk it was still snowing. And the wind had picked up, whistling around the cabin walls, blowing cold drafts down the chimney. Seeping in the cracks along with the drifting snow.

The boys huddled close to the fire, wearing their blanket coats and fur mittens. Even so, Daniel couldn't get warm. The chill wind that forced its way into the cabin seemed to blow all the way through to his bones. He kept going to the stack of wood next to the fireplace, adding another log to the fire, warring against the cold.

Warring too against the growing feeling that this wild blizzard blowing outside was too powerful for two boys alone in a small, leaky log cabin. The woods would win. Those great trees had wanted them gone from the start, Daniel thought. From the first moment he'd seen them, he had felt it. The trees, the wild varmints lurking out there among them, and now this cruel storm were too much for them. They were beaten.

No, he told himself. He couldn't think that way. He owed it to Pa and Ma and especially Will to keep fighting.

The storm had to stop sometime. They had enough wood inside to last till then, he felt sure. Daniel was thankful he'd brought in so much. But what about after that? Would they still be able to catch game with deep snow on the ground? Would their snares still work? And what about fishing? The creek would be buried under ice and snow. They would have to chop their way through it even to try.

Will had been moving around quietly, heating the rabbit stew left from yesterday.

"This will warm us up," he said.

The rich hot meat and broth did warm Daniel's insides. And it got his mind to feeling calmer too. This might be the last meal of rabbit they'd have for a while, he thought, as they scraped out the last tasty bits from the pot. Still, they had the sack of cornmeal. And the two tall piles of firewood outside. Those were the most important things. If Pa was here, Daniel knew what he'd say. With food and firewood, they could get through the harshest winter.

If they kept their heads. If no wild varmints attacked them. If . . .

He couldn't let any doubts creep in. He wouldn't.

On a stormy night like this back home, Ma would have her Bible out, reading their favorite stories to distract them all from what was going on outside. Daniel wished they had a Bible. Or any book to read.

He'd heard those Bible stories so many times, he about knew them by heart. Most likely Will did too.

"Let's tell stories," Daniel said.

Will looked at him blankly. "What kind of stories?"

"Bible stories," Daniel answered. "Like Ma reads to us. I'll start."

The way it was snowing outside like it never would

stop put him in mind of Noah and his ark. Of course, that had been rain. But it must have felt the same to old Noah.

"The book of Genesis," Daniel began, just like Ma always did. "Chapter five. Or maybe six, I can't remember. God finished creating the world and he thought it was real fine. But after a while he got angry with man on account of his wicked ways. He got so riled up, he just couldn't swallow it anymore. So finally he decided to destroy what he had made and all the creatures in it. Except for Noah.

"Noah was six hundred years old." Daniel remembered that part real clear. He'd always wondered how a man could get to be that old, and finally he had asked Ma. She said those Bible folks lived a good long time. "Seemed like he was the only good man in the world. So God spoke to Noah and told him his plan to flood the earth and drown everyone. Noah would be saved, he said, if he built himself an ark. God even told him how to build it. And he could bring his family inside and two of every living creature."

"Like cows," Will said, starting to smile. "And horses and pigs and chickens."

"And elephants," added Daniel.

This was the best part of the story when Ma told it. She would stop her reading and they would all take turns saying animals. Daniel liked to say elephants because he'd seen a picture in a book once and they were the biggest creatures to have to fit in the ark. Sarah would be sure to say butterflies. And Zeke always said frogs because he liked them best.

Daniel could see them all marching into the ark, two by two.

"So Noah did what God told him to do," he went on. "And sure enough, as soon as the ark was finished and they were all inside, it commenced to rain. It rained for forty days and forty nights. Seemed like it never would stop raining. The water covered the land so deep, the ark was floating on top of mountains."

"Forty days and forty nights," Will repeated. He looked like he was thinking what Daniel was thinking. What if it were to snow that long?

"But finally the rain stopped. The ark came to rest on top of a high mountain. Noah sat inside the ark for about forty more days and nights, waiting for the flood-waters to go down. Seemed like they never would. He sent out a dove, and it flew right back. He sent it out again, and this time the dove came back with an olive leaf in its beak, and that's how Noah knew the land was dried out."

The dove was Ma's favorite part of the story. She would pause and smile, like she was seeing in her head that white dove with a sprig of green in its beak.

"Then God spoke to Noah again, telling him he could leave the ark. So at last old Noah opened the door, and his family and all the other living creatures came walking out. And they gave thanks to God."

That was how Ma always ended the story.

Will didn't say anything for a moment and neither did Daniel. Just like those nights back home. In the quiet, Daniel thought the wind might have died down a little.

"That was a good story," said Will.

15

The sun on the snow was so bright, it about blinded Daniel's eyes. He shaded them as he looked out the cabin door into a world turned white. Everything—bushes, stumps, the two woodpiles—was buried under deep snow. All except the trees. Their branches were brushed with white, but the thick dark trunks still reached up to the sky.

Nothing moved. Not a squirrel or a bird or any living thing. The snow had frozen everything silent. It was a beautiful sight, Daniel thought. Yet he felt himself shiver. This snow was what he and Will would have to fight against now.

"How deep do you figure it is?" asked Will next to him.

After two full days without stopping, the snow was plenty deep, Daniel knew that. But it was hard to tell just how deep. The wind had blown it around so much, drifting it high here, scooping it out there.

"We'll find out," he answered.

They needed to bring in more wood. Their supply inside was running low, and it would take time for the wet logs to dry out.

Dressed in their blanket coats, their hands warm inside their rabbit fur mittens, the boys stepped out into the snow.

"Ohh!" Will sunk in up to his waist.

Daniel grabbed at him to keep him from falling down. He could barely move, he discovered, the snow weighed him down so. It seemed deepest where they were, close to the cabin. And around the two woodpiles.

The pile they were using was right next to the cabin, but suddenly it seemed far away. If only they had a shovel, Daniel thought, to dig out a path. Of course they didn't. And you couldn't chop snow with an axe. They would have to wade their way over to it.

It seemed like it took forever to reach the woodpile. Daniel's legs ached from pushing through the heavy snow. And it kept getting inside his mittens. They would have to find a way of lacing them to make them tight at the wrists. In spite of that, Daniel was surprised to find that he wasn't cold. Moving around, fighting the snow, was keeping him warm.

The boys had to brush off each log, carry it along the narrow track they had made to the cabin, then come back for the next one. After a while Daniel saw they had trampled down a path. That was good. Their next trip to the woodpile wouldn't be so hard.

"Let's rest," he suggested, after they'd brought in over a dozen logs.

Tired out, they sank down on their log chairs. As the

warmth of the fire began thawing out his clothes, Daniel noticed how wet they were. His blanket coat, his mittens, his britches, his shoes, were all soaked through. It would take hours to dry them by the fire. And while they were drying, he and Will had no other clothes to wear.

Every time they went out, it would be like this. They'd be better off staying inside, Daniel decided. At least for a few days until the snow wasn't so deep.

So they spent the next three days inside the cabin. Daniel worked on stitching together a rabbit fur hat. He thought they had enough skins now to make one, but not two. For now, they could take turns wearing it. Will started fashioning another wooden bowl. He had the idea to make one for every member of the family. And they told more Bible stories.

Will recounted his favorite, the one about Joseph and his coat of many colors.

"Joseph's father made him a wonderful coat of bright colors," Will said. "Oh, that coat was beautiful. His brothers got to feeling jealous, on account of their father liking Joseph best. They began talking mean about him and figuring ways to harm him. Some wanted to kill him, but one of the brothers said no. So they took his coat, and cast him down into a deep pit. Then some traders came along, and those mean brothers sold Joseph to them. So Joseph was taken to the land of Egypt."

When Ma told the story, Daniel always felt mixed up in his feelings. How special it must be for your pa to give you a wonderful coat like that. But how terrible for the other brothers to see Joseph was their pa's favorite. But even so, how could they want to kill poor Joseph?

"I forgot to say how Joseph was always having strange dreams," Will went on. "Down in Egypt, he got real good at telling what folks' dreams meant. He even told the king what his dreams were about. Seven years of good crops were coming, he said, followed by seven bad years. They should save up their corn for the bad years. This king, who was called Pharaoh, thought Joseph was so smart that he made him ruler of the land. After the seven good years, the bad years came. Egypt was the only place that had corn, so Joseph's brothers traveled there to buy some. And even though they'd treated him so mean, Joseph was kind to his brothers and forgave them. And he even got to see his father again."

The end of the story made them both go quiet.

"Do you think we'll get to see Pa again?" Will asked. "And Ma?"

"'Course we will," Daniel said quickly. "Seems like something must have gone wrong so they couldn't start out on time. And it would be too hard for Ma and the little ones traveling in winter. But come spring, we'll see them, you can be certain of that."

Daniel wished he was as certain as he sounded. To get both their minds off Pa and Ma, he told the story of the baby Moses.

"A different Pharaoh from the Joseph one came

along," he began. "And this Pharaoh was a cruel ruler. He ordered that all boy babies born to the Hebrews were to be drowned. But when the baby Moses was born, his ma just couldn't do it. So she put her baby in a basket, all sealed up tight, and set it afloat on the river. Well, that basket with the baby Moses inside sat in the bulrushes alongside the riverbank as nice as you please."

Ma liked this next part. She always told it real slow.

"It just so happened that one morning the Pharaoh's daughter came down to the river to wash herself. She saw the basket with the little baby inside and told her maid to bring it to her. When the princess looked down at that baby, it was crying. And she felt so bad, she saved the baby Moses from the river.

"The Pharaoh's daughter raised Moses up as her own son. And the best thing was she got the baby's own ma to be his nurse. Only after he was grown, he found out who he really was. And Moses got to be a great leader and led the Hebrew people out of Egypt."

They went through just about all the Bible stories they could remember. David and Goliath. Solomon the wise man. Jonah getting swallowed up by the whale. After that, Daniel went back to telling the stories he'd heard on his trip to the mill. Will specially liked the one about the bear hunter who lived in a big hollow tree trunk.

By the fourth day, though, Will grew restless. He always hated sitting still. And he didn't like being cooped up inside. Now he was itching to go dig out their snares.

See if they'd caught anything before all the snow fell, and then reset them higher.

"The snow's still too deep," Daniel told him. "You wouldn't even find the snares. Or be able to dig them out."

"I could find them," Will insisted. His jaw lifted in that stubborn look he got.

"We better wait till this freeze is over," Daniel answered. It had stayed cold since the storm. Trying to walk through that crusted snow would be even harder now. "A couple more days at least."

Will didn't argue any more, but he wasn't happy. He grumbled about the cornmeal mush that night. "Could be eating rabbit," he muttered to himself, loud enough so Daniel could hear.

The next morning Will was quiet. He seemed to be thinking about something while he worked on shaping his bowl. After a while he said, "Remember Grandpap's cabin?"

Of course Daniel did. It was just one room, crowded with a jumble of guns and traps, old tools and fishing gear. Since Grandma died, he never straightened it up.

"What was on the wall by the fireplace?"

In his head Daniel saw it clear as could be. Snowshoes. Now he knew what Will was thinking about. If only they had those snowshoes, they could get around outside.

"Seems like we could make us some snowshoes," Will said. "I've been studying on how to do it."

He scratched a rough picture on the dirt floor with his

knife. It looked simple enough. A long triangle shape with the wide end forward and a piece across the middle where a shoe could be attached.

"All we need is two long sticks of wood and two or maybe three shorter ones," Will explained. "And some plant fiber to tie them together."

It could work, Daniel thought. They might as well give it a try. If they could move about on top of the snow without sinking in, they'd no longer be at the mercy of the winter weather. They wouldn't be stuck inside the cabin, but could try some trapping, maybe some fishing.

From their supply of kindling, the boys chose two straight, strong sticks for the long part of the triangle and three shorter ones for the crosspieces. Will laid them out on the floor so they looked just like his drawing. Then, with his knife, he notched all the ends so they fit snugly together. After that, he lashed the pieces together with plant fiber.

Just like Pa would do, Daniel thought. If you needed something, you found a way to make it yourself.

It wasn't long before the first snowshoe was finished. It was a strange shape, not like Grandpap's rounded ones, and it didn't have webbing across the inside like his did. Daniel's first thought was that this couldn't work. They were wasting their time. Still, if there was a chance that this stick triangle would keep them on top of the snow, they ought to try it.

Daniel thought they would make just one pair and try them out. But Will was so sure they would work that he kept going. By afternoon, Daniel and Will had four rough-looking snowshoes. The hard part came next. How could they attach them to their feet so they wouldn't step right out of them?

That turned out to be not as hard as Daniel expected. They simply stood on the middle crosspiece and wound plant fiber around the shoe and snowshoe till it felt tight and strong. Then they were ready to try them out.

Will went first. He took one step into the deep snow and began to sink. Just as Daniel had feared, this wasn't going to work.

But then, just as the snow covered his moccasins, he stopped sinking.

"They work!" he shouted.

He took a second step, and fell sideways into the snow.

Daniel had to bite his lip to keep from smiling. Will looked like a stranded fish lying there.

"I tripped myself," he said.

Will struggled to his feet. As soon as he tried to walk, however, he tumbled over again.

"One foot keeps stepping on the other one," he told Daniel.

But the snowshoes weren't sinking down. At least not very far. That was a good sign.

Daniel decided to try it himself. He climbed out of the narrow path that led to the woodpile into the deeper snow. The snowshoes felt strange, like some kind of big, clumsy duck feet. Looking down, though, he saw that like Will, he was standing almost on top of the snow.

Carefully he moved one foot forward. Then the other. And fell over just like Will had.

"Ha!" Will grinned down at him. "See, it's not so easy."

No, it wasn't easy. The snowshoes kept getting tangled up, one on top of the other, sending Daniel toppling over again. He floundered awkwardly, trying to stand up. When Will attempted to help, they both went down together. Cold wet snow got inside Daniel's mittens and down the neck of his coat. But he was surprised to find he didn't care. For the first time since Pa had left, or maybe longer than that, he and Will were laughing.

Finally, almost at the same moment, they got the hang of it. The secret, Daniel discovered, was to keep his legs far enough apart so the snowshoes didn't bump into each other.

It was a new way of walking. All at once, Daniel could move. He was free of the heavy snow that had weighed him down, kept him trapped inside the cabin. Now he and Will could roam the woods as they had before, walking on top of the snow.

They tramped around, making triangle-shaped tracks in the snow. Will did a strange little dance. Daniel scooped up snow and threw it at him. They couldn't stop smiling. It felt so good to be outside again.

Will's cheeks were bright red from the cold, but his eyes shone.

"Let's go check our snares," he said.

FEBRUARY

16

The snares were empty, buried deep under the snow. Daniel wasn't surprised at that. But he was surprised to see tracks in the snow, quite a lot of them. Rabbit tracks, some smaller ones that he thought might be weasel or marten, and even smaller, feathery wisps of tracks. A bird? A mouse? And the sharp, clean hoofprints of a deer.

So it seemed there was game to be had, if they could just catch it.

If only they had Pa's gun, Daniel thought longingly. With one shot, they could bring down a deer. And a deer had so much meat on it, it would last for many days, weeks even. Then they wouldn't have to be worrying about snares or spears.

But they didn't have Pa's gun. They had to reset their snares.

Daniel and Will worked carefully, setting the snares higher and concealing them as best they could with handfuls of snow. Stepping back, Daniel could barely make out their outlines against the vast sea of white.

"We'll catch some rabbits," Will said confidently as they tramped on their snowshoes back to the cabin. "I know we will."

He went out to check their snares every day. But every day he returned empty-handed.

"Maybe all those tracks belonged to one rabbit," he said.

"One smart rabbit," added Daniel.

The weather warmed some. The snow melted, dripping off the cabin roof. Then it rained for a whole day, melting more of the snow cover. The boys went out and reset their snares again. Still, day after day, Will returned without a rabbit dangling by its ears in his hand.

Maybe, Daniel thought, something was wrong with their snares. It could be they stood out somehow against the snow. Or maybe he'd been right in thinking of rabbits sleeping away most of the winter in warm burrows.

Whatever the reason, it was going on two weeks, he figured, since they'd had anything to eat besides johnny-cake and mush. Daniel found himself hungry most of the day, a gnawing, empty feeling. He'd even started dreaming about food. Ma's chicken and dumplings, smothered in gravy. Her pumpkin pie. One morning he woke up sure he smelled it baking. When he saw Will stirring the pot of cornmeal mush as usual, he was so disappointed, he could barely crawl out of bed.

The creek, which had been frozen solid, began flowing again. That gave Daniel a new idea. Why couldn't they try fishing once more? Not with Will's spear this time, but with homemade poles and lines made from plant fiber. And hooks carved out of bits of wood. That way there'd be little chance of Will falling into the freezing water again.

Will didn't take to the idea. He was proud of his spear and proud of his skill at catching fish with it.

"You can use a pole," he said, frowning. "I'll stick to my spear."

No, you won't, Daniel vowed to himself. Not while the creek bank and everything else was covered with a slick coating of snow and ice. But he said nothing.

That night Daniel worked at carving fishhooks out of small splinters of wood. It was hard to get the right size and shape, and he threw most of his efforts into the fireplace. Finally he got one that he thought might work, shaped from the branching Y of a twig. By that time, the light from the dying fire was growing dim. Daniel's eyes were tired, and his fingers ached from holding the tiny bits of wood.

"I'll do better in the morning," he said.

As usual, Will went right to sleep while Daniel lay awake, thinking. He wondered if the hook he had whittled would really work. He'd need to tie on a stone to weight the line, he reminded himself. That made him think of Pa and how he could always invent something to solve a problem. Maybe he and Will were starting to do that. Starting to be like Pa.

That led Daniel to another thought. One of those days that he'd stopped counting, not too far back, had been his birthday. January 14. He hadn't given it a thought, but he was twelve now, just about grown. Some days he didn't feel like it at all. More like a toddling babe trying to cling to his pa's shirttail. Other days he felt full grown. In fact, sometimes downright old.

Would Pa be proud of him if he could see him now? Daniel wondered. The thought brought an unexpected wave of homesickness that made him ache all over. What were Pa and Ma doing right this minute? And the little ones. Shy, serious Sarah. Round-faced Abby, always smiling. Funny Zeke. And the baby, probably crawling under everyone's feet by now. If they were all still alive.

They had to be. He'd know somehow if they weren't, wouldn't he?

Daniel lay still, trying to bring their faces to mind. Strange, he could see Pa all right, and Ma. Small and bony thin, always bustling about like a fluttering bird. He could never forget the wide smile that would unexpectedly light up her face. But the little ones were fuzzy in his head. Sarah, Abby, Zeke. Their features seemed to float just out of reach.

He was slowly floating into sleep, the faces blurring into swirling clouds of snow, when a sound outside brought him back. A sound of running. Some wild critter in the snow, it must be. No, more than one. Wolves chasing their prey? Most likely, he thought.

They were close to the cabin. Daniel sat up. He heard something thrashing about, some kind of struggle. Moments later, a muffled crash. Then silence.

If it was wolves, whatever they'd been chasing, they had caught.

It was over. Daniel settled back beneath the blanket.

As he was drifting off to sleep again, he heard another sound. High and long, echoing through the trees. And, a moment later, an answering call from somewhere nearby. Once the sound would have made him shiver. Not now. The wolves are singing, he thought.

And he went off to sleep.

Next morning Will set off to check their snares, while Daniel took out his knife to work some more on the fishhooks. But before he had even chosen a likely bit of wood, he heard a shout outside.

"Daniel! Come and see!"

Daniel opened the door and looked out.

Will was standing at the edge of their clearing. The first thing Daniel noticed was blood on the snow. A large, dark stain. Then he saw a deer lying next to it. No antlers. A doe. Good-sized. Dead.

So that was what he'd heard last night. Wolves chasing a deer out of the trees, running her till she was so exhausted she couldn't run anymore, then bringing her down. Right here, almost next to the cabin.

"I'm coming!" he called to Will.

Putting on his snowshoes, Daniel trudged over to where the deer lay. As he got closer, he saw that the wolves had eaten their fill before leaving. The back legs and belly of the deer were torn up, a lot of her insides gone. But so much was left. Compared to a rabbit, a deer was a mountain of meat.

He and Will looked at each other.

"Meat!" said Will. He was grinning so hard, his face looked like it might split in two.

"Tons of it!" Daniel grinned back.

He was amazed at their good fortune. No need now to think about fishhooks or rabbit snares. They had meat to last a good long time.

They had to get it to the cabin, though. And soon, in case the wolves returned or some other varmint with a taste for meat came along. Looking at the deer, suddenly Daniel realized something else. It wasn't only the meat they could use. The hide too was valuable. For clothing, shoes, laces, and probably much more. Solomon had been dressed all in deerskins, he remembered.

So the two boys set to work skinning the deer. It was harder than Daniel expected, much harder than skinning a rabbit. It took hours before they finally had the hide separated from the meat. They laid it out on top of the second woodpile to dry. And it took more hours to chop up the meat with the axe and their knives. Some they buried under the snow, in a kind of box beneath the woodpile. There it would stay frozen and, Daniel hoped, no wolves would find it. The part they could use right away they brought inside.

Then they couldn't wait any longer. They cut strips of meat and roasted it on sticks over the fire. The venison smelled so good cooking, they didn't even wait for it to be cooked through.

"It's ready!" Will said eagerly.

They devoured it, red juices dripping from their chins. Almost like wolves themselves, Daniel thought, looking at Will's face. Maybe people weren't so different from wild critters after all, even though they wore clothes. Like every other animal, they had to eat. And spent the best part of their lives struggling to do it.

Oh, that deer meat tasted good! Better than rabbit. There was more to it, like it would go right into the blood and build up a body's strength. Neither of them could stop grinning as they finished off those first pieces of meat and cut more. For once, they didn't have to stop eating till they wanted to.

And they didn't. The boys gorged themselves till Daniel thought he couldn't eat another morsel no matter what. He was stuffed so full, he felt like his belly would split open if he tried to move. Will lay back, still smiling, as if he'd never stir again.

"Tomorrow we'll make a stew," said Daniel.

"A big one," Will answered sleepily.

"We can use the bones and fat for soup," Daniel added. After that, maybe, the bones could be used for something else. Some kind of tools, like the Indians made?

"And there's the hide," Will reminded him.

Yes, there was the hide too. The deer was a gift, Daniel thought, a wonderful gift. Except for Solomon, it was the best thing to happen to them since Pa left.

17

It snowed and they ate deer meat. For days on end, it seemed, that was all that happened.

No more big storms came like that first one, just small snowfalls no deeper than the length of Daniel's knife blade. But they kept coming every three or four days, piling up until the snow on the ground was as deep as it had been before the thaw.

Daniel and Will stayed inside. They had no need to go out, not even for water. All they had to do was fill the iron pot with snow and melt it over the fire. They had plenty of meat, so they didn't have to think about resetting the rabbit snares or trying out Daniel's fishing pole. Their supply of firewood was holding up too. They had just started on the second pile, so it was pretty sure to last till spring. And despite the chinking that had fallen out and several small leaks in the roof, the boys were mostly fairly dry and warm in the cabin.

They kept busy. Daniel had been thinking off and on about school ever since the talk at the horse mill that day. He feared he and Will were in danger of forgetting all the book-learning Mr. James had taught them back home. So he scratched verses he could remember from their primer into the dirt floor. "In Adam's fall we sinned all." "Zaccheus he did climb a tree his Lord to see." He had Will copy them. And he wrote out arithmetic problems for them both to solve. He tried to make it into a game, but Will didn't much want to play. He'd never been strong on book-learning.

Daniel worked some more on his fishhooks. After a while he got the hang of shaping them, and made a supply of hooks. They might not need them now, but one thing he'd learned in the months they had been alone was to plan for later. While he carved his tiny bits of wood, Will set himself to making a large, heavy spear.

He'd been talking about it a long time. He had the wood picked out, a straight, strong length of tree limb wider around than his fist and taller than he was. Now Will worked on it like he had his fishing spear, taking off the bark, scraping away the knobs, sharpening the end to a point.

"It's not really for hunting," he told Daniel, "but for fighting off wild varmints. Like wolves."

"Or bears," said Daniel.

Will frowned, looking down at it. "The point isn't strong enough," he said. "I wish I had a sharp piece of metal. Like my knife."

"You can't use your knife for a spear point," Daniel objected. "We need it."

They needed their knives for so many chores each day. From eating to carving to skinning to making clothing.

Along with the axe, their knives were the most valuable tools they had.

"I know," answered Will. "Maybe a sharp stone would work."

A sharp stone could work, Daniel thought. Only where would they find one under all this snow?

"When the snow melts, we'll look for one," he said.

In the meantime, Will worked on his spear point until it was as sharp and strong as he could make it. When he finished, he set the spear next to the axe beside the cabin door. Daniel hadn't thought about a weapon to protect themselves from wild varmints. He'd only wished for Pa's gun. But he had to admit it was a comfort to see the spear standing there.

They brought in the deer hide from the woodpile and let it thaw and dry out for a few days. While it was drying, Daniel tried to decide what they could best use it for. A deerskin shirt? Britches? Another pair of moccasins? His own shoes were starting to wear thin like Will's had. And shouldn't they cut at least part of it into thin strips to make stronger straps and laces? The plant fiber worked well for many uses, but it wasn't strong enough for everything. Like attaching their snowshoes. They had to keep redoing them every time they went outside. And sometimes the fiber broke, forcing them to wade back to the cabin.

In the end, it was the stiffness of the hide that made Daniel decide. That and the fact that it had been so ripped up by the wolves that there wasn't a whole lot left that they could use. As it dried, the hide had become almost as hard as a wooden board. Thin and tough, but difficult to bend even a little bit. How could they cut and shape it into any kind of clothing? And even if they did, how could they bear to wear anything so stiff? Daniel knew there was a way of softening it. The deerskins Solomon had worn hung loosely from his shoulders, he remembered. And the moccasins he'd made for Will were as soft as they were strong.

You had to soak the hide, he thought. Probably for several days. That much he remembered from listening to Grandpap, who had hunted and trapped every kind of animal. Then stretch it out somehow and scrape off all the hair. All of that would have to be done outside. But how? Daniel could imagine doing it in warmer weather, but not in the cold and snow. And after that would come the job of cutting it into a shirt or britches or moccasins and sewing it together.

It seemed too hard. He studied on it, but no new idea came to him. So finally, thinking this was probably a mistake, that he ought somehow to be turning the hide into clothing, Daniel decided to cut it up for straps and laces.

That night he set to work. Carefully, trying hard not to waste any, he cut the hide into long, narrow strips. The strips were still stiff, too stiff to use for snowshoe straps, so he tried rubbing one of them between his fingers. This seemed to soften it a little. Then he found that rubbing it over a stick of firewood worked better and faster.

Will helped, and after a few nights of work, they had a small pile of softened strips of hide. Not as soft as Will's moccasins, but good enough, Daniel thought.

So the next day they tried out the snowshoes with their new straps.

It had snowed lightly again that morning, but by mid-afternoon the sky was a bright, clear blue and the sun was shining. The sunlight gleamed on the fresh, unmarked snow. Even the trees had a more friendly look, it seemed to Daniel, their dark branches outlined in white.

The moment he stepped out onto the snow, he could tell that the new straps were going to work. They stretched with each step he took, but didn't break. And they felt comfortable around his ankles.

Will thought so too. As soon as they'd brought in a new supply of firewood, he said, "Let's go look at the creek."

Walking down to the stream, they checked the thickness of the ice. Then they circled back to search for their rabbit snares, buried deep under the last few snows. They looked for fresh tracks, and saw a few rabbit ones here and there. Also a set of larger, rounded prints.

The boys bent down to study them.

"Wolf," said Will right away.

Daniel nodded. For the first time, he found himself

thinking of wolves in a friendly way. Was this one of those that had brought them the deer? he wondered.

The tracks were close together and not mixed with those of any other animal.

"Not chasing anything," Daniel decided. "Just passing by."

Look close. You see.

Finally, as the sun began to sink behind the trees, the boys tramped back to the cabin.

Inside, they left their snowshoes propped against the wall by the door, next to the axe and Will's new spear. Will poked up the fire and started heating last night's venison stew. As the good hearty smell of meat filled the cabin, Daniel suddenly realized how hungry he was. All that tramping about had given him a bear's appetite.

He looked around at everything lined up along the cabin walls. The sack of meal, still more than half full. The little pile of deer-hide strips waiting to be used, along with a tangle of plant fiber. The extra blanket. The fishhooks, heaped in one of Will's carved bowls. And outside, frozen underneath the snow, still plenty of deer meat.

For the first time, Daniel felt pretty sure of it. They were going to make it through the winter.

MARCH

18

The first thing Daniel heard in the morning, before he even opened his eyes, was the dripping. All through the day, it went on without stopping. And it was the last thing he heard before he fell asleep at night.

The snow was melting.

It dripped off the roof. It dripped from the trees and the woodpile. It dripped through the holes in the roof onto the dirt floor, turning it muddy. The boys had to scurry about, catching the worst drips in Will's wooden bowls and emptying them out the cabin door.

Every day the blanket of snow on the woodpile grew smaller. Here and there in the clearing, patches of bare ground began to show. A day came when they no longer needed their snowshoes. They hung them up, like Grandpap did, on the wall next to the fireplace.

They finished the last of the deer meat. After all that good venison, it was hard to think about going back to rabbit and fish, but Daniel couldn't see any way around it. It seemed unlikely that the wolves would bring them another gift of a deer. And there was no way they could hunt or trap such a large animal themselves. So the boys set out their rabbit snares again.

Now that the snow was melting, they saw more creatures moving about in the woods. Everywhere, it seemed, the round white tails of rabbits popped up. Daniel caught occasional glimpses of raccoon and possum, and once, the bright fur of a fox. Squirrels darted on the ground and in the treetops. Birds flitted and pecked. One, with a red head, kept up a loud drumming on a hollow tree behind the cabin.

It didn't take long to catch their first rabbit. And their first fish.

Will insisted on taking along his fishing spear as they walked down to the creek.

"The ice must be melted by now," he said.

But it wasn't. It was much thinner, though. Sitting on the wet log that was half in, half out of the water, Daniel found it easy to chop a small hole and let down his hook, baited on the end with a scrap of rabbit meat.

Now all he had to do was sit and wait.

Will paced restlessly on shore, his eyes to the ground, his spear held ready in his hand.

"What are you looking for?" asked Daniel.

"Don't know," Will mumbled. "Frog maybe. Or turtle."

"Too early," Daniel told him. Back home it would be late spring before they heard frogs croaking in the nearby pond. "They're still sleeping under the mud."

Will stubbornly kept looking. He wandered downstream while Daniel sat quietly on the log, jiggling his line now and then.

All at once, the line jiggled by itself. Startled, Daniel pulled it out of the water. On the end, caught by his homemade hook, was a small, squirming brown fish.

"I got one!" he called to Will. "Our hook worked."

The hook worked perfectly. Daniel caught a second fish, this one a little bigger. Just enough for their dinner, he thought. Only this time the fish had swallowed the hook. When Daniel tried to pull it out, the hook broke. That was the end of his fishing for today. It didn't really matter, though. He'd caught their dinner, and they had a lot more hooks back at the cabin.

Will came back from his wandering, his hands empty except for his spear. But he had an excited gleam in his eye.

"Tracks!" he exclaimed. "You have to see them."

He led Daniel downstream to a place where the melting snow had turned the creek bank to mud. Kneeling down, they both looked.

"I think it's a turkey," Will said.

The tracks were clear on the muddy bank. A bird, because of the three clawlike toes. And a large one. Daniel remembered the size of the turkeys he'd seen on the way to the mill. It sure did look like a turkey.

The two of them studied the tracks for a long time, following them into the woods, just like Solomon would, until they couldn't make them out anymore.

"One turkey," Daniel said finally. "Must have strayed away from the rest."

A turkey would make a mighty fine meal, if they could catch one.

They talked about it as they walked back to the cabin. And later, as they ate the fish Daniel had caught. The fish were crisp and tasty, cooked in a little rabbit grease in the frying pan, but Daniel didn't feel filled up like he had with the deer meat. Next time he'd have to catch three or four.

Will turned quiet after they finished eating. Daniel knew by now that meant he had latched on to something in his mind. And he knew to keep silent while his brother worked it out. Sure enough, in a little while Will started poking a stick into the dirt floor, drawing something.

After he stopped making marks, Daniel asked, "What is it?"

Will grinned. "Turkey trap," he said.

It would be made of logs from the woodpile, he explained, built in a roughly square shape. On one side would be a low opening, just large enough for a turkey to get in. Once inside, Will was pretty sure it wouldn't be smart enough to figure how to get out.

"What's going to make it go into the trap?" asked Daniel.

"We'll lay down a trail of johnnycake," Will said.

Daniel wasn't so sure the turkey wouldn't find its way out. But, as with the snowshoes, it seemed worth a try. All they could lose was some meal, and they had plenty of that.

They set the trap nearby, building up the logs almost like they had when they put up the cabin. And, like the cabin door, they left an opening on one side, just large enough for the turkey to get in, but low to the ground. Then they sprinkled crumbs of johnnycake from the edge of the woods all the way into the trap.

Once again Daniel thought of Pa. Even he might not have thought of this kind of trap.

"It could work," he said.

Will seemed sure of it. "It will," he said confidently. "You'll see."

He couldn't wait to check the trap the next morning. While Daniel was cooking up their breakfast mush, Will hurried outside. When he came back, he looked dejected.

"No turkey," he told Daniel. "And no johnnycake. The birds or squirrels must have eaten it."

They hadn't counted on that. Still, Daniel couldn't think of anything else they could use for bait.

"We'll just have to keep trying," he said.

So every day they laid down a new trail. And every morning, when Will went to check, he found no turkey and no johnnycake.

"Maybe we should give up," Daniel said after several days went by. "All we're doing is feeding the birds and wasting our meal. Most likely that turkey is long gone."

They hadn't seen any more tracks when they went to the creek.

151

Will frowned. He never liked to give up on anything.

"One more day," he said.

"All right," Daniel agreed.

He was picking out a new hook for fishing, when he heard something outside. A strange noise, somewhere between a yelp and a cluck.

"What's that?" he asked.

Will didn't answer. He was already out the cabin door, racing toward the turkey trap. Before Daniel could follow, he heard Will shouting.

"We got it!"

The turkey had no notion of how to get out of the trap. Will had been right about that. It paced around, squawking and gobbling indignantly. Daniel felt sorry for it. At the same time, he was noticing how much bigger it was than the chickens back home, how much meat it would provide them.

Seemed like one creature always had to die so another could live.

They waited till the turkey tired itself out. Then they threw a blanket over it and dragged it to a nearby stump. And, just like Pa did with the chickens, Daniel chopped off its head with the axe.

For the next few days, all the boys ate was turkey. They had it roasted over the fire and then cooked up into a stew. Even the bones boiled in water made a delicious soup. It made Daniel think of Ma and the soups she made, filled with vegetables and sweet herbs from her garden. Maybe when spring really came, he could find wild greens to add to the soup pot.

Too soon the last of the turkey soup was gone. Will went out once again to check their rabbit snares, while Daniel wandered down to the creek to try some fishing.

He'd just settled himself on the log and let his hook down into the water when he had the feeling someone was standing behind him.

"Will?" he said.

Turning, he saw it wasn't Will but someone taller. For just a second, he thought it was Pa. But no, Pa didn't wear deerskins.

"Solomon!" he said.

19

It was so good to see Solomon standing there. Just as before, he seemed to have simply appeared out of the woods. He looked exactly the same, straight and tall and still dressed in his deerskins, as if it had been only yesterday that they'd said good-bye.

"White boys are catching fish?" Solomon spoke as if it really had been yesterday.

"Not today," Daniel answered. "But other days."

He brought up the line to show Solomon his homemade hook.

Solomon nodded. "Good hook. It catches many fish."

Daniel felt warmed by his praise. But he found himself strangely tongue-tied. It had been so long since he'd spoken to anyone but Will.

Solomon spoke instead. "Where is brother?" he asked.

"Will went to check the rabbit snares," said Daniel.

"And Papa and Mama? They come?"

Daniel shook his head.

Solomon looked at him silently for a long moment. "So white boys alone all winter."

"Yes." Daniel saw that Solomon was gazing at his blanket coat. Suddenly his tongue came untied.

"We made these coats. And mittens from rabbit fur. And Will figured out how to make snowshoes. And then the wolves killed a deer right by the cabin so we had all that meat and the hide too." He was babbling now, spilling out everything that had happened since last fall.

Solomon listened quietly, nodding every now and then. When Daniel finally stopped for breath, he said, "Boys learn. That is good."

He hadn't called them white boys this time, Daniel noticed. Maybe they had earned a little bit of the Indian's respect.

Will appeared, carrying a dead rabbit by its ears. His face lit up at the sight of Solomon. He wasn't tongue-tied at all, but immediately showed him his moccasins with their rabbit fur linings.

"They're the best shoes I ever had," he said. "My feet were warm all winter."

"*Tschi mammus* is small," said Solomon. "But he gives much. Meat and fur."

Daniel wanted to ask so many questions. Why was Solomon here? Had he come to do more trapping, or maybe just to see if he and Will were all right? How long would he stay? But he knew Solomon would tell them whatever he wanted them to know in his own time.

He didn't ask, and Solomon told them nothing more that day. Soon, with a wave of his hand, he disappeared into the trees.

For two days the boys looked for him, but he did not

appear. They did some more fishing. The ice in the creek had finally melted, and the water was running fast. Again and again, Daniel let down his line, but nothing seemed to be biting. Will, fishing spear in his hand, was about to step into the cold water, when a quiet voice behind them said, "*Cla hi can* catch more fish."

What did that mean? Daniel wondered.

"A trap?" said Will. "For fish?"

"I show you how," said Solomon.

He showed them how to make a trap of thin sticks, woven together so that one end was wide and the other closed. He placed the open end in the water at a place where large rocks narrowed the creek, creating little riffles between pools.

"Fish swim in. Cannot get out," Solomon explained.

Daniel understood. Why hadn't they thought of that? Just as with the rabbit snares and turkey trap, they could have this fish trap working for them while they did other things.

As he had last fall, Solomon would suddenly appear and, as suddenly, be gone. Some days he talked to the boys and even made one of his small jokes. At other times, Daniel noticed, he hardly spoke at all, as if some dark mood had crept over him.

The days grew warmer. The last of the patches of snow melted quickly, and Daniel noticed tiny buds beginning to appear on some of the trees. Soon those buds would turn into leaves. And everywhere he looked, bits of green were poking up out of the ground. Plants seemed to be lifting themselves out of their long winter sleep.

Some of those plants could be eaten, Solomon told them. One afternoon he walked with the boys through the woods and along the creek, picking up a leaf here, slicing a root with his knife there. Daniel remembered a few of the plants from Ma's kitchen. The wild onion, which Solomon called *wi nun schi,* looked different but smelled just the same as hers. Most, though, he'd never thought of eating. Like the ferns that had just started to spring up next to the creek, and the tiny violets that were popping out everywhere. Now they would have greens to add to their next rabbit stew.

Solomon also pointed out poisonous plants.

"Bad in the belly," he said, holding his stomach in such a comical way that both boys had to laugh. But they stopped abruptly when he added, "If you eat it, maybe you die."

He showed them healing plants as well, wild herbs and roots. *Beson,* Solomon called them, which Daniel decided must mean medicine. The bark of certain trees could be boiled in water to make a curing drink, he told them, or applied to the skin to heal a wound. Pointing at a butternut tree, he said, "This fixes pain in the head. Or tooth."

Daniel wondered if these remedies would really work. But Ma had her own cures, made from herbs like feverfew for headaches, hyssop for coughs, and tansy tea for stomachache. Maybe these weren't so different from hers.

After that, many days went by without their seeing

Solomon. Once again, Daniel was concerned that something might have happened to him. But then he dismissed his worry. In some strange way, he thought, Solomon reminded him of Pa. They were both so strong and certain about things, and both knew so much. Solomon was part of the forest. Nothing in it could harm him. He would be back.

He came again on the warmest day yet. The sun was shining, and the boys hardly needed their blanket coats. For the first time, Daniel could make out the soft green of new leaves on the little dogwood tree near the cabin. He saw more splashes of green all around them, breaking up the dull brown of winter, as he and Will walked down the path to check their fish trap.

They were in luck. Two small trout and a crayfish were caught neatly inside the trap, unable to find their way out. As Daniel removed them, he noticed that one side of the trap had come apart. He dragged it out and started reweaving it, while Will looked around for sharp rocks. He was determined to make a good point for his large spear.

This time Daniel sensed Solomon's presence before he spoke. He turned around just as the Indian stepped out of the trees.

"Ah," said Solomon. "Good." A suggestion of a smile flickered across his face. "Boy hears like Indian."

That was about the highest praise he could give, Daniel knew.

But today Solomon seemed different. Tired, and the

lines in his face appeared to have grown deeper. It occurred to Daniel that he might be as old as Grandpap. Solomon watched without speaking as Daniel tied together the fish trap and set it back in the water. He showed Will how to make a spear point by tapping one rock against another, breaking off small pieces until, finally, he got the sharp point he wanted. However, he seemed distracted, as if his thoughts were somewhere else.

At last, as Will sat patiently chipping away at his rock, Solomon spoke.

"I go find my old home," he said, gesturing upstream. In the direction of the horse mill, Daniel thought. "Once upon a time, a big village was there. Many houses and canoes and horses. This was good land for hunting. Plenty of deer and beaver, fox and bear. And so many fish, they jump out of the water into your hand. I wished to see it one more time." He stopped for a moment, and Daniel saw that his eyes were filled with sadness. "All is gone now. Trees grow up. Nothing is left. Only this."

Solomon opened his hand and showed them a small, broken bit of blackened clay.

"Part of cooking pot," he said.

Daniel suddenly remembered the two men at the mill, Jake and Sam, boasting about their pa and uncles driving away the Indians. They could have been talking about Solomon and his village.

He didn't know what to say. Even Will was silent, still chipping at his rock, his head down. Daniel had never

159

imagined that whole villages had once stood here in the woods. From everything he'd heard back in Pennsylvania, this Ohio land was unsettled. That was why Pa had come here, wasn't it? And if that wasn't so, if the Indians had been here first, why did they have to be driven out? In these vast woods, wasn't there enough land to share?

"I'm sorry," he said finally. It didn't seem like enough, but he had to say something.

Solomon shook his head. "Boys did not burn our houses. Did not kill my father and brother. Old people and babies too."

He stopped speaking, looking off into the trees as if he was seeing once more what had taken place there long ago. Then he went on. "My heart is bitter a long time. I want to kill white men. Kill his father and brother. Kill many like they killed us."

Daniel could picture that younger Solomon, his eyes gone hard, his body lean and strong, stealing through the woods to take his revenge.

"Now," Solomon continued, his voice quieter, "I have no more anger. My heart is only sad."

There seemed nothing more to say. Daniel stared at the little bit of clay pot in Solomon's hand, trying to imagine how he would feel if that was all that was left of his village.

The three of them sat a few minutes more. Then Solomon rose slowly to his feet. With his customary small wave, he disappeared into the trees of his old home.

APRIL

20

Solomon left them two days later. He said good-bye to the boys standing outside the cabin.

"I go back to my people," he said. "Cannot stay in place that makes my heart sad."

Daniel felt his own heart sink. He'd just started not feeling alone, and now Solomon was leaving them again. Will's face looked long too. Just a moment ago he had been jubilant, showing Solomon how he'd attached his spear point to the heavy shaft with tight strips of deer hide.

The Indian seemed to sense their feelings.

"Boys have good house," he told them encouragingly. "Catch many *tschi mammus*, many fish. The time of planting comes soon. You chop trees. Put seed in the ground. Raise plenty of corn."

Daniel nodded. Now that the hard winter was past, they would be all right, he was pretty sure. It was just that they'd be alone.

"Will you come back?" Will asked, his voice sounding almost pleading.

Solomon hesitated a moment. "Maybe, at the time of hunting," he said. He stopped, then added, "Maybe Solomon's bones are too old."

163

Daniel thought of Grandpap and how he talked about his poor old bones aching in the cold and damp. And he thought of how far Solomon had to walk. He had no idea how many miles, but surely his journey was many days. Maybe he wouldn't come back.

Suddenly he wanted to give Solomon something.

"Wait," he said, darting inside the cabin.

His eyes ranged around the small room, seeing the two cooking pots, the meal sack, the blankets, the bowl filled with fishhooks, another with deer-hide strips. What did he have to give anyone?

The cup he had carved sat on the rough table. It wasn't much, but it was all he could think of. Daniel picked it up and hurried outside.

"Take this," he said, holding it out. He felt a bit foolish. A poorly carved cup was so little to give after all Solomon had given them. "We thank you for—" He waved his hands awkwardly. "Everything."

Solomon took the cup, turning it over slowly to look at each side. "Boy made this. Good."

Once more Daniel felt a little flush of pride.

And then, without another word, Solomon walked away.

As he was about to disappear among the dark tree trunks, Will called out, "Good-bye!"

Solomon turned. He waved briefly, and then he was gone.

All the rest of that day Daniel felt something heavy weighing him down, sinking his spirits. It wasn't just Solomon's leaving. He'd known that would come, though he'd hoped not so soon. It was something else. It wasn't until that night, as he lay wrapped in his blanket staring into the flickering fire, that he figured out what it was.

Not once since the first day had Solomon said a word about Pa and Ma. It was as if he knew they were never coming.

Was that what Solomon thought? He'd spoken as if Daniel and Will were going to be chopping down trees and planting corn by themselves. And was that what he—Daniel—thought?

He didn't really know what he thought, he realized. All winter he had pushed the family out of his mind, just dealing with what he and Will had to do to survive. He'd known deep down that Pa wouldn't be traveling in such harsh weather. But now spring was coming on. Mightn't they be setting out now? Whatever had gone wrong last fall should be fixed by now. Unless, of course, what had happened was so terrible that he would never see any of them again.

Daniel was afraid to get his hopes up only to see them dashed again. The thing to do, he decided, was not to count days or keep watching for Pa and Ma. Not even to talk to Will about it. The two of them needed to do exactly what Solomon had said. Chop down trees and make a field for planting corn. That was what Pa had planned to do come spring. He'd talked about it so many times. Of course, Pa had had other plans too, grander ones, like planting a field of wheat as well and buying a cow and maybe some pigs. Pigs could live in the forest, foraging for themselves all summer, and then you'd have them to slaughter for meat in the fall.

One thing at a time, Daniel told himself, his eyelids drooping at last. First, the trees.

Chopping down the trees to make a field was not going to be an easy task. With the axe in his hand, Daniel looked around him the next morning. Why, some of those trunks were so wide around, so massive and hard-skinned, he and Will hadn't a chance of cutting them down. With their gnarly branches, their odd-shaped knobs that looked like bony knees, they reminded him of the granddaddies they were. The axe would bounce right off those tough old hides. Even the smaller ones, those he could reach around, would be days of work. They had only the one axe after all, and he and Will were nowhere near as handy with it as Pa.

Many a day he'd watched Pa cutting down trees for the cabin. Daniel knew well enough how it was done. And he'd cut down saplings, and chopped firewood for hours on end. But he had yet to bring down a full-sized tree by himself.

"We'll start here," he told Will.

166

They stood by the south side of the cabin, near the spot where they'd found the deer killed by wolves. At home, fields were some distance from the house. But here, they'd plant close by. That way they could use the start of a clearing Pa had already made. And on this side of the cabin, Daniel calculated, there were fewer giant trees.

He picked out a tree to start with. Not a really big one, but fair-sized. A young elm, he thought it was. Daniel pictured Pa in his mind. The first thing he would do was cut a notch in the side of the tree. The side he wanted it to fall. No question, that was away from the cabin. With a few half-swings, he made his notch. Now he could just swing away.

"Stand clear," he said to Will.

Daniel brought back the axe. He coiled himself up like he'd seen Pa do. Then he swung from his heels.

But somehow his curled strength didn't travel straight up to his hands the way Pa's did. The axe head was heavy. It threw him off balance, and he came close to falling over. Looking up, he saw that the axe had barely bitten into the tree.

Daniel felt silly. He looked over to see if Will was laughing at him. Thankfully, he wasn't.

"Guess I ought to slow down," he muttered.

His next swing wasn't so hard. Daniel saw a small chip fall to the ground. He kept swinging, and pretty soon he began to feel a rhythm to it. Stand back, look at the tree,

167

take aim, swing. Stand back, take aim, swing. Chips flew. Slowly the cut in the tree became deeper.

After a while, though, Daniel's arms began to ache. His back and shoulders were sore. His swings slowed down, and he could see that the axe head wasn't biting in as far. Finally he had to stop and rest.

He leaned on the axe handle and wiped his damp forehead with his shirttail. Looking sideways at the cut he'd made, he could see it wasn't as deep as he'd thought. Not near deep enough to fell that tree.

"My turn!" said Will eagerly.

He had trouble too to start, but he kept at it like Will always did, slowly deepening the wound in the elm's side while Daniel leaned his back against a nearby tree to rest.

Then, when Will started slowing down, Daniel took up the axe again. They went on like that all morning, taking turns chopping and resting, and it seemed to Daniel that they'd never get through that tree trunk. If it was Pa swinging the axe, he'd likely have two or three down by now.

They stopped for a drink of water and slabs of johnny-cake. Daniel was feeling so puny, he needed something to build back his strength. Though they were both too tired to talk, Will's face told him he felt the same. The food and short rest helped. In a few minutes Will was back up and reaching for the axe.

"Ready?" he said.

He took his turn chopping, then Daniel did again,

thinking about how long these trees had stood on this spot without anyone bothering them. Rooted side by side, standing shoulder to shoulder, their branches interlacing in a friendly sort of way. It was no wonder they wouldn't go down easy.

But he could be stubborn too. They were going down. They had to, to let in the warm sun, to make a place to plant so that he and Will, the intruders, could live too.

Starting with this tree.

Daniel swung the axe with new energy. He was starting to get the hang of it now, he thought. Planting himself firm, gathering all the power he possessed from his feet and sending it upward to his arms, then out through the sharp head of the axe. Like Pa, maybe.

He didn't feel tired anymore, just determined to conquer this enemy. He swung and saw the gash grow deeper and wider, and swung some more, and finally he sliced into the heart of the tree. It swayed.

Daniel looked around to see where Will was standing. "Stay back," he warned.

He swung again. The tree stayed upright.

He swung once more. The elm leaned slowly toward the giant next to it, brushing the broad trunk with its branches like it was saying good-bye. And it fell.

"We did it!" Will shouted. "Hurrah!"

He climbed up on the fallen trunk, waving his arms triumphantly.

Daniel set down the axe. Now that it was done, it

seemed like all the strength had drained right out of him. He was so tired, he could barely stand.

He looked at the tree he and Will had brought down. It didn't seem like the enemy now. It sprawled broken on the ground, its trunk appearing somehow small, its top branches still upright, leaning against its neighbor's trunk. On the tips of the branches, new leaves were just unfolding.

Daniel felt a fleeting sadness for those leaves that would never grow out. For taking their life.

But it had to be done.

"That's the first one," he said, picking up the axe.

21

They kept chopping, day after day.

Early each morning Daniel took up the axe and he and Will set about their day's work. Choosing a tree, cutting it down, chopping up branches, dragging them away from the planting field they were starting to make. That was hard work too, especially when they were tired from swinging the axe. They had to climb over knee-high fallen tree trunks and jagged stumps. Someday all of that would be piled up and burned, but there was no time now, even if they'd had the strength to do it. They had to get the clearing made so they could plant this spring.

"Then we'll walk to the horse mill and see about getting some seed corn," Daniel told Will. "You can come with me this time."

Will grinned at that. And for the next few minutes he chopped even harder than before.

The granddaddy trees they didn't try to bring down. Daniel knew better than to think he could. Instead, they girdled them like Pa had done last fall, making slashes in the tough bark in a circle all around and leaving them to die in their own time.

Daniel got to feeling like the axe was part of his hand.

When they finally quit in the late afternoon, he was so tired and his shoulders ached so badly that he could barely drag himself back to the cabin. He sank down in the doorway and just sat there, imagining in his mind the ragged, slowly-growing clearing as it might be someday. No giant logs, no stumps jutting up every which way, but a broad, flat field waving green with new corn.

Will's energy never ran down for long. Soon he'd be practicing with his new, heavy spear, throwing it at a stump.

"When we go to the horse mill, I'll take it along," he said. "In case of wolves or bears."

Then he would go off to check the rabbit snares and the fish trap. Most days Will came back carrying something for their supper. But if not, Daniel hardly cared. He was just as happy to eat a bowl of cornmeal mush before falling into a heavy sleep next to the fire.

Some mornings when he awoke, he could hear a quiet rustling in the trees outside. Like they were whispering to one another, *Which of us next?* But of course, that couldn't be so. It was only a little breeze skittering among the new leaves.

Overnight, or so it seemed, all of the woods had turned green. It was like it had happened while they were sleeping, Daniel thought. Spring was really here. Buds had turned to leaves, ferns had begun to uncurl their featherlike fronds, new plants popped out of the ground where nothing had grown yesterday. The little

172

dogwood behind the cabin was about to burst into bloom. Dogwood was Ma's particular favorite. She loved to see them blossoming pink and white in the woods and along the roadsides each spring. He was going to spare that little dogwood, Daniel had decided. Maybe someday Ma would be able to look out her cabin window and see it blooming.

This day was almost like summer. The rays of sun that found their way into their clearing seemed to have burned away the early spring chill. The sun felt good on Daniel's shoulders as he swung the axe. The air smelled of earth and green growing things. Birds swooped and sang in the trees. Red ones, yellow ones, a fat blue one with a reddish chest. *"Too-ree!"* they warbled. *"Per-chick-o-ree!"*

It was hard to keep your mind on your work on such a day. By mid-afternoon, Daniel couldn't do it anymore. It was all right to give themselves a break every now and then, he told himself. Not that Pa ever would. But they needed to rest their aching shoulders so they could pick up the heavy axe again tomorrow.

"We could go down to the creek and look for greens," he suggested to Will. Will had come back with a nice fat rabbit yesterday, and that had set both of them to thinking of Ma's good stews.

"And maybe have a swim," Will added.

A swim would be good. Daniel hated to think how long it had been since they had bathed. Ma would be scandalized if she knew.

"I'll take my spear and practice on the way," Will said.

So Daniel picked up the bucket and Will carried his spear.

They found a few young ferns, the ones Ma called fiddleheads, growing close to the water. And here and there, patches of tiny violets. Also, the low-growing, broad-leafed plant Solomon had called whitefoot because, he said, it grew everywhere the white man walked. The boys picked handfuls of each and dropped them into the bucket.

"We need wild onion too," said Will.

Ma always had onion in her delicious stews. Daniel tried to remember where they had found it the day they'd walked here with Solomon.

"I think it grew away from the creek," he said.

They walked along, eyes searching the ground. Daniel spotted something he thought might be wild onion. He stooped to pull it up, sniffing at its roots. It didn't have that strong onion smell, and he thought of Solomon's warning about poisonous plants. Better let it be.

He stood up to show it to Will. But his brother had walked on, his back bent, the spear resting on his shoulder.

Daniel was about to follow when he saw another plant at the base of a maple tree. Two long, oval leaves with a thin stalk starting to grow up between. This looked like the plant he remembered. He rubbed a leaf between his fingers, then smelled his hand. Onion! He'd found it.

More plants grew on the other side of the tree. And another patch behind it.

"Will!" he called.

No answer. Had Will wandered off again without thinking? Didn't he remember the time they'd gotten lost? Or had he started practicing throwing his spear and forgotten all about looking for wild onion? How could he be so careless?

"Will!" he cried again.

Daniel thought he heard something from the direction Will had been walking. Not a call, but something. He followed the sound, calling Will's name as he went. But he got no more answer.

Then he heard another sound, one that made him stop and jump behind a big hickory tree. The growl of some wild critter. A large one, and close by. Bear? Or panther, maybe? Wild cats had roamed these woods a long time ago, Pa had said, but he'd seemed pretty sure they were gone now.

Daniel edged around the broad trunk. Cautiously, he peered out.

A large bear, shaggy-black and looking thin after its long winter sleep, stood on its hind legs next to a small tree. Its front paws rested on the tree's narrow trunk. Its mouth was open, and Daniel could make out sharp, yellowish teeth. As he watched, the bear growled again as if in a fury and swiped a long claw at something above.

The tree leaves moved, and suddenly Daniel saw what

the bear was trying to reach. Will sat huddled in the tree's low branches.

All at once Daniel's heart was pounding wildly in his ears. He wanted to shout, to try to drive the bear away. But he knew he should keep quiet. He was no match for an angry bear. His mind raced. What should he do? He had no weapon, just a bucketful of greens. If only he'd brought along the axe! He could run back to the cabin and get it, but that would take so long. Will was in too much danger.

Now the bear shook the tree, as if it aimed to rattle Will out. Like shaking down nuts. The thin trunk swayed. Will swayed with it, clinging desperately to his branch. For a moment he seemed about to fall.

Then he scrambled higher into the tree's branches. Daniel could see that he couldn't go much farther. The tree was too small, its branches too weak. They would break.

The spear! Where was it? Daniel's eyes roamed over the ground. There it was, not far from the tree. Most likely Will had dropped it when he started to climb.

If he could just get to the spear. Then what? Should he attack the bear? Was the spear strong enough to kill such a large animal? Solomon had helped make it. It would be strong enough—if Daniel was. But the bear was so big and so angry. Maybe he should just try to distract it until Will could jump down and they could both escape.

First he had to reach the spear. Daniel began working his way toward it, taking care to stay behind the bear so it wouldn't catch sight of him. Will knew Daniel was there, that was plain. He made no sign, but leaned out of the tree, taunting the bear, making sure to keep its attention.

Careful, Will, thought Daniel as the bear once again raked its claws high up the tree trunk.

He inched closer, crouching behind some straggly bushes. He could make out the spear clearly now, its stone point looking sharp and dangerous. Just a few more steps and he could reach out and grab the shaft.

Daniel didn't know how it happened. He'd been so careful, moving as silently as Solomon among the trees. His foot came down on a dead branch, hidden beneath a blanket of moss. And he heard a sudden, sharp crack.

The bear turned. The small eyes in its great black head stared at Daniel, as if trying to make sense of what they saw. For a moment, nothing moved. Then Daniel heard a low roar as the bear loomed up in front of him, its fur long and matted and stuck with bits of bark, its open mouth dripping saliva, its little black eyes glittering with rage.

"Watch out!" Will cried.

No time to reach the spear. No time to run or climb a tree. Wildly, not knowing what he was doing, Daniel flung the bucket of greens at the bear's head.

Everything after that happened in a blur. The bucket bounced harmlessly off the bear's shoulder. Enraged even more, the bear swiped at Daniel with one powerful paw. Then somehow Daniel was rolling on the ground, aware of nothing but terrible pain and the knowledge that he was about to die. Dimly he made out the dark, awful shape coming after him once more. The long, sharp claws, the teeth. He couldn't move. Something was wrong with his leg. Helplessly, he waited for another blow.

It didn't come. The shape was on top of him, heavy and suffocating and smelling of everything rank in the woods. And then, miraculously, it wasn't. Daniel heard a sound—*whoooshh*—like a long, hard sigh, and the next thing he knew Will was shaking his shoulder.

"Can you get up? You have to. Daniel!"

Daniel tried to move. Waves of pain rolled over him.

"Can't," he mumbled.

Where was the bear? What had happened?

"Bear's not dead—only wounded. Have to get out of here—before it wakes up." Will spoke in short bursts, all the while lifting Daniel under his arms, dragging him, causing more pain.

The pain was everywhere. Ribs, head, back, but mostly his left leg. He couldn't walk. He had to. Before the bear woke up.

Daniel struggled to stand. Looking down, he saw torn britches and something red running down, dripping onto the ground. Blood. His blood. So much of it. All at once his head started spinning. His stomach churned. Then he saw the bear. It lay slumped on its side under the small tree, its eyes half closed, the spear shaft sticking up just behind its shoulder. More blood—the bear's—made a dark, growing stain on the ground around it.

Its huge chest heaved. No, it wasn't dead. At least not yet.

Somehow, with Will supporting him, Daniel was walking. Limping, dragging his bad leg, dripping blood, but walking as fast as he could toward the cabin. Will kept him going, letting him lean heavily on his shoulder and talking without stopping.

"Come on, Daniel. That's right, lean on me. You can make it. Keep going. We're almost there."

Now and then he looked back.

"Nothing's following us," he reassured Daniel. "And it's not going to, 'cause that bear's as good as dead. I got him with my spear."

Despite everything, pride was in Will's voice.

Step after painful step, Daniel hobbled along. It seemed to take forever before the cabin finally came into sight. Will almost carried him through the door. And then he was lying on his bed of leaves, lying in a pool of blood and pain.

Daniel felt woozy. The room seemed to be spinning around. He closed his eyes, but it wouldn't stop its whirling.

He felt Will touch his leg and the pain rose up, hot and red, making him cry out. "No!"

"I have to," Will said softly. He worked at the thin cloth of Daniel's britches with his knife, peeling it away.

Daniel heard a faint ripping sound, then silence. And Will's voice again.

"Your leg," he said. "It's hurt bad."

MAY

22

"Eat this, Daniel."

It was Ma's voice, quiet and gentle, urging him to eat. Just like she always did when he was sick with a belly-ache and she brought him one of her special soups.

"It's good. Taste it."

Ma was here! Just like in his dreams. He had been sleeping—it seemed like he slept so much lately—and while he was asleep they had finally come. Now he could rest and let Ma take care of him and Pa finish cutting down the trees. So many trees. In his worst dream, giant trees were pushing up out of the cabin floor.

"Wake up, Daniel."

Daniel opened his eyes and saw Will's face, not Ma's, close to his own.

With a stab of disappointment, he looked around the cabin. No Ma or Pa. They hadn't come while he was sleeping. It was just the two of them, as always.

Will's forehead was wrinkled, like he was worried about something. His hand held a wooden spoon close to Daniel's mouth. "You need to eat," he said.

It wasn't like Will to be worried. Obediently, Daniel opened his mouth. Warm broth trickled down his throat.

Broth from a rabbit stew. Not like one of Ma's special soups, but it tasted good.

"You've been hot with fever," Will told him. "And sleeping all the time and talking crazy about trees. You wouldn't eat. And your leg. It looks bad."

While he talked, Will spooned in more broth and bits of tender rabbit meat. Daniel felt himself growing a little stronger, more awake. He lifted himself up on his elbows.

"How long has it been—" Daniel stopped. He couldn't say the words.

"Since the bear attack," Will finished for him. "Three days now."

Closing his eyes, Daniel could see it all over again. The enormous black head with the little bright eyes, the dripping mouth, that swift swipe of a paw, startling in its power, which had sent him rolling end over end on the ground. And after that, the terrible curtain of pain coming down. It was so unreal that even now it felt like a dream. The worst one ever.

"That bear clawed your leg real bad," Will went on. "And now it's all swelled up and red and it's not getting better."

Daniel didn't want to look, suddenly afraid of what he might see. But he knew he had to. He gazed down at his leg. As Will said, the whole leg was an angry red, and swollen to near twice its size. It no longer even looked like it belonged to him. And just below the knee were deep, ragged gashes, torn by the bear's sharp claws. He remembered the fierce pain he'd felt at first. Now it was just a constant, throbbing ache.

He could tell from the redness and swelling that the leg was starting to putrefy. This was bad. Folks had a leg cut off sometimes from wounds like this. If it wasn't cut off, they might die.

Once Pa got kicked by a horse. Not old Ben, but the feisty, copper-colored mare they'd called Penny. Pa had a knot big as a goose's egg on his ankle and it wouldn't go down. Ma tried all her remedies. Finally the doctor had come all the way from two towns over, and he'd given Pa a salve to rub on it. Even that didn't help, and they began to despair. But then Ma made up a new poultice from wild herbs she dug in the woods, and little by little the knot went down.

Ma's herbs. That's what Daniel needed now.

They didn't have them. Or a doctor to ride over. Or Solomon.

Solomon. The day he'd shown them plants that could be eaten, hadn't he pointed out healing ones as well?

Will seemed to have the same thought at the same time.

"Now that you're awake, I'm going to find something to help," he said, jumping to his feet. "You rest till I get back."

Just the effort of sitting up had tired Daniel. He lay back, falling into another doze. He didn't know how long it was before he was roused again by Will's voice.

"I think I found it," he said, not sounding as certain as

he usually was. Daniel saw he was carrying strips of tree bark. Yes, he remembered Solomon telling them something about tree bark as a cure.

"I'm not sure if it was the right tree," Will went on. "But if this doesn't work, I'll get more bark from more trees."

Now he sounded like himself. So determined, he'd likely pull the bark off every tree around.

Will boiled up some water in the big pot, then dropped in the bark and stirred it around. Daniel had seen Ma do this dozens of times, making one of her poultices.

"Do you think it's ready?" Will asked.

It had only been a few minutes. Daniel didn't know how long Ma steeped her cures, but he recalled her stirring a long time.

"Not yet," he said.

Will let the bark steep awhile longer. In the meantime, he looked around till he found a scrap of cloth left over from their blanket coats. He covered the cloth with meal, spooned the liquid from the pot over it, and folded the wool into a small, wet bundle. He brought it over to Daniel.

"This might hurt a little bit," he said.

That was what Ma always told them when she doctored their scrapes and bruises. Will must have heard it a hundred times, he got so many.

Daniel tried to smile. It *did* hurt, so much, he came

near to crying out. But after a few minutes, he found that the damp heat felt good, like maybe it was drawing out the poison from his leg.

"Now you rest some more," Will told him.

He changed the poultice many times that day. By the next morning, Daniel thought the swelling might have gone down a little. He dragged himself over to the doorway so they could look at his leg in the sunlight. Maybe they were just being wishful, but it seemed a little better, though the dark gashes were still puffed up and oozing.

"More poultices," said Will.

Over the next few days, he took care of Daniel just like Ma would have if she'd been there. Each morning Will inspected the injured leg and made up new poultices. True to his word, when he wasn't satisfied the wounds were healing right, he went out and gathered more bark from different trees. He checked the rabbit snares and the fish trap. He brought back greens to add to the stews he cooked, and fed them to Daniel until he was strong enough to feed himself. He cleaned up the cabin, sweeping the floor with the hickory broom. He even sewed patches on Daniel's britches.

Daniel was amazed. This was a new Will, not restless, headstrong, everlastingly ready to argue, but patient and gentle. He didn't ever complain, though Daniel could see sometimes by his slumped shoulders how tired he was.

In the evenings, Will told stories. Bible stories again, the same ones they had told each other during the long, snowy winter. But after a few days, the story Daniel most wanted to hear was of the bear attack.

"I just about stumbled over it," Will began. "My head was down, searching for wild onion, and I looked up and there it was."

He seemed a little sheepish. No doubt he was recalling everything Solomon had taught them about watching and listening. Daniel opened his mouth to remind him, then remembered that he too had paid no mind that day to anything but plants.

"The bear was tearing at a rotten stump, looking for insects. It came at me so fast, I just climbed the nearest tree. Soon as I did, I knew it was a mistake. I'd picked too small a tree. And the bear was bent on getting me out of it, one way or another."

"Did you hear me calling you?" Daniel asked.

"I heard, but I was scared to answer. I was afraid of stirring up that bear even more. So I kept quiet, hoping I could hold out in the tree till it got tired and gave up."

Daniel wondered if that would have happened. Maybe, if he'd done nothing, the bear would just have wandered away and there wouldn't have been an attack. But how could he do nothing when it looked like Will would be shaken out of the tree into the bear's jaws any second?

"Then I saw you," Will went on, "and I knew you'd seen the spear and were going after it. So I tried to distract the bear, but then it spotted you. Throwing the bucket at it was good. It slowed the bear down long enough for me to jump down and grab the spear. I attacked it from behind just as it went after you. You know what happened after that. The bear was hurt pretty bad, but so were you. I had to get you out of there. Wish I'd killed it, though."

Daniel remembered the bear lying on its side, the spear sticking out of its back. Its blood soaking the ground.

"Maybe you did kill it," he said.

"Could be." Will's eyes brightened. "I ought to go see. If it's dead, I could get my spear back. And a bearskin besides."

That was the old Will, ready to jump into anything without thinking it through. What if the bear was still nearby, not dead, and made even angrier by its wound? What if Will got himself into some other kind of danger and Daniel couldn't rescue him? If something happened to Will too, who would take care of them?

Daniel felt uneasy. At the same time, he knew Will was going to do it. He had to. In his place, Daniel had to admit, he'd likely feel the same. So all he said the next morning was, "Take the axe. And keep your eyes open."

Will nodded. "I will."

As soon as he left, time seemed to slow to a crawl. Daniel could move around a little now, enough to change his poultices and keep a small fire going. But he still couldn't stand long on his injured leg. He busied himself working on the new cup he'd started to carve, all the while listening for Will's footsteps.

The morning crept by. Daniel's fingers grew tired of carving. He got up and put more wood on the fire. He nibbled on a bit of johnnycake left over from breakfast.

Why didn't Will return? Surely he'd had enough time now to find the place of the bear attack and come back. Images of the bear, so dark and fearsome standing on its hind legs, floated inside his head. He could almost feel again the powerful cuff of its paw that had sent him flying as easily as Daniel could swat an insect.

Then all at once Will was standing in the doorway. Safe, uninjured.

"I found our bucket," he said, holding it out. Remarkably, it too seemed undamaged. "But that's all. The bear was gone."

Daniel was so relieved, he hardly heard Will tell how he had crept up, as quiet as Solomon, to where the bear had been. Seeing and hearing nothing, he moved closer. He saw where the bear had lain, the ground still bloody and torn up. No spear, but, looking around, he found the bucket in the underbrush. Looking closely at the muddy earth, he made out tracks. Bear tracks.

"So I followed them," Will said.

Daniel's heart sank. Pursuing any wounded animal was dangerous. And an already angry bear most of all.

"Will—" he started to say, but Will interrupted.

"Maybe it was foolhardy," he admitted. "But I was

careful. I wanted to see if I could get back my spear. I followed the tracks to the creek, and then downstream a ways. After that, they faded out and I lost them. Guess that bear is long gone."

Once again Daniel felt a wave of relief. Will would always be Will, that was clear. Maybe, though, someday he'd get a lick of sense. Maybe he was even starting to.

Will was frowning.

"Now I'm going to have to make me a new spear," he said.

23

Will began working on a new spear shaft that night. Over the next few days he finished it, and Daniel completed his new cup. He thought he'd done a better job this time. The shape was rounder and the carving smoother.

"Wish I could give this one to Solomon," he said.

Will nodded. "I know. My new spear's going to be better too."

He went out searching for the right rock to make his new spear point. When he returned, he had three sharp-looking rocks to try. He also brought back long strips of bark that he'd peeled from trees. But not for poultices this time.

"I was thinking we could maybe use it for making boxes," he said. "Or baskets."

It would be useful, Daniel thought, to have boxes for storing things in the cabin, like the fishhooks and deer-hide strips and plant fiber. And they could use baskets for gathering greens and nuts and berries, and for carrying fish. Now all they had was the bucket. So the boys set themselves to making a box out of hickory bark.

They bent a long strip of bark into a round shape. Then they cut out a flat circle piece to make the bottom of the box and another like it for the top. They poked holes and laced the bottom to the sides. The first one they made came out badly, lopsided and ill-fitting. Will was so disgusted, he threw it into the fire. But the next day they tried again. And again, until finally they had a box that satisfied them.

Will gathered up the fishhooks and put them into the box. He set it on a thin slice of wood that he'd fitted between two logs in the corner, like a shelf.

"There," he said. "Almost looks like home."

Daniel knew what he meant. Ma stored supplies in pantry boxes in the kitchen back home.

The next afternoon they worked on fashioning a basket for carrying things. It was a warm day, almost summerlike again. Daniel hated to be inside, though he knew he was still too weak to go out.

Will began by soaking strips of bark so they would bend more easily. Then the two of them started folding them into a rough basket shape. When they got the shape they wanted, they would make a line of holes along the edges and sew the pieces together with deer-hide lacing. And last of all, they would add a bark handle.

It was slow, tedious work. The boys ruined more strips of bark than they were able to bend into shape. After a while, Daniel noticed that it was growing dark inside the cabin. Could it be supper time already? It didn't seem like they had been working that long.

"What was that?" asked Will.

Daniel had heard it too, a low faraway rumble.

"I don't know," he said.

Suddenly the darkness was pierced by a bolt of white light. Then, a minute later, they heard a louder rumble.

"Storm coming," said Daniel.

A breeze picked up in the trees outside. More lightning flashed and thunder grumbled. A few minutes later, rain pattered on the roof.

In moments it came pouring down in torrents. Water began dripping in the holes in the roof, forming bigger and bigger puddles on the dirt floor. Will moved their half-shaped basket to a dryer spot close to the fire. But then rain splashed down the chimney, making the coals sputter and go out.

The storm raged on. Flashes of lightning lit up the cabin for an instant, then it turned black as night again. The crashes of thunder were so loud, they seemed to rock the earth underneath them. The wind was shrieking now, blowing so hard, Daniel was afraid the bark roof might blow off. Though he couldn't see them, he knew the tops of even those granddaddy trees of the forest were bent by its power. They too could come crashing down.

This was as bad as the winter blizzard. It made Daniel feel small, at the mercy of angry, too-strong forces outside. He thought of what he and Will had done then.

"How about telling some stories?" he asked.

Will spoke up right away, his voice quieter than usual, but steady.

"I could tell the one about Daniel and the lions' den," he said.

Ma used to tell that one over and over, seeing as it was about a man named Daniel. But when Will told the story now, it sounded different.

"Daniel was a good man," Will began. "He prayed to God three times a day. But then some bad men talked the king into making a new law, that you couldn't pray to anyone but the king. So, for punishment, Daniel was cast into a den of lions. And a great big stone was rolled over the opening so he couldn't get out.

"Those lions," he went on, "were the fiercest critters you ever saw. Like giant cats. Big as bears, but yellow colored. They had mean eyes and terrible teeth and claws sharp as knives. One, the biggest of them all, the king of the lions, stood up on its hind legs and roared like thunder. Oh, it didn't look good for old Daniel."

Daniel remembered how scared he'd felt when he first heard this story. He hadn't known what lions were exactly, but they sounded real bad.

"But Daniel, he wasn't afraid. No, sir. He drew himself up tall as he could, and looked that king of the lions right in the eyes. And what do you think happened then?"

Daniel knew what happened. But he said, "What?"

"Why, that great big fierce lion lay down and started purring like a kitty cat. And so did the rest of them. And when the king had the stone rolled back from the lions'

195

den, there they were, Daniel and all those lions, peaceful as you please."

That wasn't quite the way Ma told it. In the real Bible story, it was God who saved Daniel from the lions, not Daniel. It seemed like Will was making Daniel sound braver than he was. And there was no king of the lions in the story either, on its hind legs roaring like thunder.

Could it be, Daniel thought, that Will was trying to say something about him and the bear attack?

Daniel didn't think he'd been brave. He just did what he had to do. It was Will who'd been brave like he always was, attacking the bear with his spear. Was following the tracks of a wounded bear brave or was it foolhardy? Or both, maybe? Was it brave to do something you had to do, while shaking in your shoes with fear? Had Will been afraid when he sunk his spear into the bear's back? Could Daniel have done that?

So many questions made Daniel's head spin. The only thing he was sure of was that he and Will were easier with each other now.

And one more thing. Telling stories made you forget what was going on outside. The rain was starting to let up a little, he noticed. The thunder sounded farther away.

He smiled. "That was a real fine story," he said.

24

Daniel's leg was healing. Thanks to Will, thanks to Solomon, thanks to Ma, he thought. The swelling and redness had gone down and the torn flesh was beginning to knit together. He could stand now, for longer and longer each day. It was time to get back to work.

Past time, he thought. His injury had cost them many precious days, days when they should have been chopping away at their clearing. It ought to be finished by now. As the days kept growing warmer, Daniel could feel it. This was the time to be putting seeds into the ground.

He picked up the axe.

"What are you doing?" Will stared at him, startled.

"We have to get back to cutting down trees," Daniel said, "so we can plant our corn."

"What about your leg?" Will protested. "You can't stand on it for long. And you're still weak. You better rest a few more days. I'll start chopping."

Will sounded like a fussing mother hen. Like Ma, almost. Who would have thought it?

"Time's wasting," said Daniel. "We'll do it together, like before."

But he had to admit that the axe seemed heavier than

he remembered. His arms felt pretty near as weak as his legs. That came from lying around the cabin so long. Well, he wasn't going to be lying around anymore.

Determined, he marched outside, picked out a likely walnut tree, and started chopping.

It felt good to be outside, the sun beating down warm on his shoulders, the smell of some woodland flower tickling his nose. The dogwood he thought of as Ma's tree was in full bloom now. A pink one, it was. And it felt good to be swinging the axe again.

At first it felt good. Daniel was amazed at how quickly he tired. One minute he was chopping, and the next he had to sit down quick before both legs gave out under him.

"Guess you better take a turn," he said to Will.

Mostly that day he sat and watched while Will did the best part of the work. Daniel took his turn, but he found himself wearing out almost as soon as he started, his legs and arms weak as water. Will went at the tree like he did everything else, stubbornly nicking away at it, refusing to give up even when Daniel could see his thin arms beginning to shake. He was bent on taking down that tree before the day was out. Only Will didn't have the strength of Pa, or even of Daniel. He couldn't do it on his own.

"We have to stop," Daniel told him finally. The light was fading from the sky. And Will was having trouble standing.

Reluctantly, he dropped the axe.

"I'll bring it down tomorrow," he said.

They both limped to the cabin and sank onto their log chairs. For a long time they just sat, unable to move enough to poke up the fire and cook something for their supper.

Discouraged, Daniel thought about how much still had to be done before they could plant. Six more trees, at least, needed to be taken down. He'd calculated that while he was resting that afternoon. He guessed by how warm it was that it must be the middle or end of May. If they didn't get their corn in the ground soon, it wouldn't ripen before frost. Will couldn't do it all by himself. Daniel had to get stronger, and fast.

He couldn't help the next thought that came creeping into his head. If only Pa was here. Oh, wouldn't he bring down those trees in a hurry! Pa and Ma. He'd been thinking about them a lot lately, he realized. But he hadn't allowed himself to think of their coming. That was because, he thought with a sudden twinge of pain, he knew. If they had set out in early spring like he'd hoped, they'd have been here by now.

They weren't coming.

Daniel swallowed hard, forcing the thought away.

"Guess we better fix some supper," he said.

The next day wasn't much better. On top of the weakness in his legs, Daniel's shoulders were sore from the day before. He felt useless watching Will chop doggedly at the walnut tree, scowling fiercely at it, willing it to fall. At last, late in the morning, it did. Will barely paused to look at it before moving on to tackle the next tree.

Daniel worked at dragging off the smaller, lighter branches that had fallen into the clearing. At least he could do that. By the end of the afternoon, though the second tree hadn't come down, he felt like they had made a little headway.

Slowly, day by day, he felt his strength returning. He could stand longer. His arms were growing used to swinging the axe again. Soon, Daniel thought, he'd be able to take his full turn at chopping.

One morning they awoke to hear rain beating down on the roof. Water was dripping in through the leaky places, making puddles on the floor. Looking out the door, Daniel's heart sank. The sky was a dull gray, the ground muddy and sodden. And the rain looked like it wouldn't be stopping any time soon. Now they would lose another day.

After breakfast he was surprised to see Will pick up the axe, like he did every day now.

"Where are you going?" Daniel asked.

"We can't let a little rain stop us," answered Will.

That was just like him, to keep going no matter what.

"Wait," said Daniel. "Think, Will. The ground is muddy out there. What if you slip and fall? Or drop the axe on your foot? Or worse?"

"I'll take care," Will said.

"If Ma was here, she'd say you'll catch your death of cold," Daniel persisted. "If something happens, I'll have to take care of you and we'll lose even more time. It's not worth the chance."

Will had his stubborn look now, the one Daniel dreaded seeing. His brow was furrowed, his mouth set.

"I won't catch cold," he muttered.

Daniel took a deep breath. "You're not going," he said.

Will's face reddened. He glared at Daniel. "I am."

Daniel took a step closer to him, holding out his hand. "Give me the axe," he demanded.

Will's hand tightened around the axe handle, but he made no move. Neither did Daniel. For a long moment, their eyes locked together. Daniel could see a struggle going on inside his brother's head. Then, very slowly, Will released his grip on the axe.

"Guess maybe it's not worth the chance," he said.

A lick of sense. Could be it was coming.

The day of rain was a blessing, it turned out. The boys rested and ate the young rabbit Will had found in one of their snares, cooked with a pot of greens. They worked a little on another bark box and on Will's spear head. They ate large slabs of johnnycake, then rested some more. And when it cleared late in the afternoon, they went for a swim in the creek.

The next morning Daniel felt pretty much like his old self. His leg was just about healed. He could swing the axe again without tiring. He was ready to take his turn, and maybe Will's as well. With new resolve, he set himself to chopping down a good-sized maple.

They brought down that tree in the afternoon, with a crash that splintered the top of the one next to it. That made three of the trees Daniel'd had in mind to come down. Three more to go.

"If we cut down one tree each day," he told Will, "we could finish in just three more days."

"We'll do it." Will's narrowed eyes and lifted chin showed no doubt.

He went at the next tree in a whirlwind of flailing arms. The axe head flashed in the sun. Chips flew. The *thwack* of iron biting into wood rang through the forest, over and over without slowing. Daniel just about had to pry the axe handle out of Will's fingers to take his turn.

By evening that tree was down. Two more.

Then one.

The last of them, a hickory, was the hardest, it seemed to Daniel. As steadily as he and Will chopped, they made little headway. The axe head appeared almost to bounce off the tough skin of the hickory. It was stout, this old tree, and stubborn. It meant to keep standing.

Inside his head, Daniel once more heard a whisper. *You can't take me. I won't go down.*

You will go down, he answered fiercely.

Tiredness was seeping into his arms again. Will had begun to slow down too. But they kept chopping. Until finally, with a groan that seemed nearly human, the tree shuddered and then came crashing down, shaking the ground beneath their feet.

This time Will made no move to climb up on that thick gray trunk in triumph. Daniel was too tired even to smile. He leaned on the axe, barely able to stand upright.

"Looks like we're ready to plant," he said.

JUNE

25

Daniel stood in the cabin doorway, looking at their new clearing in the bright morning sun. Despite his and Will's hard work, it wasn't as large as he'd like. Not near the size of the fields Pa worked back home. Not only that, but it was barely a clearing at all, spotted as it was with ragged stumps and logs too heavy to move and those grand-daddy trees that would take their time dying. Under the ground, he knew, were tangles of crisscrossing roots that would trip any plow that tried to loosen the soil.

If they had a plow to loosen the soil.

Still, he told himself, it was a start. They would plant corn among the stumps and maybe grow enough to sell so they could buy a horse. With a horse, they'd pull up stumps, pile logs to burn, and improve the clearing so they could plant more corn. And sell it to buy a milk cow. And then chop more trees to make more of a clear-ing so they could plant a little wheat. And someday they'd have a farm.

He'd like a horse like old Ben, Daniel thought. Sturdy and patient and calm.

"Are we going?" Will's impatient voice spoke up behind him.

"'Course we are," Daniel answered.

This was the day they were walking to the horse mill to try to get seed corn. Daniel didn't know if the miller would give it to them, seeing as they had nothing to pay him with and owed a debt already. But maybe they could trade work for corn. He and Will were getting mighty good at chopping trees.

"Time to get started," Will urged.

He was so excited, he could barely contain himself. Finally he'd get to see something beyond their clearing and the creek. Daniel couldn't blame Will for that. And he was itching to meet other settlers like the ones Daniel had told stories about, and maybe hear more stories for himself.

He'd finished his new spear and was taking it along.

"In case of danger," Will said.

Daniel knew that meant bears.

They'd best be on their way. Daniel wrapped some slabs of johnnycake to eat on the journey, then picked up his knife. He took a last look around the cabin for anything they might offer the miller in trade for corn. Snowshoes? Bowls? Fishhooks? No, there was nothing.

"Let's go," he said.

They had just stepped out the door, when Will asked, "What was that?"

Daniel had heard it too. A high cry from somewhere in the woods. Most likely some animal pouncing on another, he thought. They'd heard that often enough.

"Must be a wild critter," he said. "Maybe a turkey."

They had only taken a few steps when they heard the sound again. Louder this time. Closer by. It almost sounded human.

Then Daniel caught sight of something moving, coming toward them out of the trees. A small figure. Human. Running and shouting.

"Daniel! Will!"

For a moment Daniel was too stunned to understand. The figure was a boy, but who? He didn't look familiar. This was like something from one of his dreams. Then he heard Will shouting too.

"Zeke!"

The next moment the boy had flung himself at them, still shouting, laughing, knocking Will off his feet. Why, of course. It was Zeke, their little brother! And behind him came others. Daniel recognized them now. Sarah and Abby, his sisters, grown bigger than he remembered. Sarah held the baby, much bigger, in her arms. And after that, Ma—yes, Ma was all right!—and then Pa.

They were all alive! They were all here!

It was almost too much to grasp. Pa looked like he couldn't believe his eyes either. He was clapping Daniel on the shoulder, smiling the broadest smile he could remember.

"You're alive!" he exclaimed. "Thank God!"

Ma had her arms wrapped around both boys at the

same time, hugging them hard. Daniel thought she'd never let go.

At last she leaned back to look at them.

"Are you boys all right? My, you look fine! Oh, thank the Lord! We've been heartsick with worry about you all these months."

Will spoke up, asking the question in Daniel's mind before he could get it out.

"Why didn't you come?"

Tears welled up in Ma's eyes, spilling down her cheeks. "It was the sickness kept us so long," she answered, dabbing at her eyes.

"What sickness?" Daniel asked.

Pa spoke up then. "Your ma was taken real bad with the fever. And then it was winter, and after that I was laid low. Try as we might, it seemed like we couldn't get strong enough to start out."

So that was what had kept them. For the first time, Daniel noticed how thin Pa looked, like he'd shrunk inside his clothes. His bones showed where they never had before. His wrists were knobby, his jaw sunken. And his face had a strange grayish color.

As if he had read Daniel's thoughts, Pa straightened up. "We'll talk more about that later. What about you boys? Are you really all right? It pained us so to think of you alone out here all winter."

"We did fine," Daniel told him. As he said it, he realized it was true.

Abby was staring at him, her eyes large in her round face. "What happened to your britches?" she asked.

Daniel realized how ragged he and Will must look, their shirts tattered, their britches torn and patched.

"They wore out," said Will.

Ma didn't seem to care. "Never mind," she said, smiling now. "We'll make new ones."

Then they were all talking at once, asking questions.

"Are there neighbors nearby?" Sarah wanted to know.

"Not for miles," said Daniel.

"Is this our cabin?" Zeke gazed up at it, his eyes puzzled. "It's so little."

"It's only a start," Pa told him. "We'll make it bigger."

Daniel longed to ask his own questions. How bad was this sickness that had held them up so many months? Was Pa well now? But he would have to wait. First, they had to see the cabin.

Pushing aside the blanket door, Daniel suddenly felt shamed by how it must look to them. Specially Ma. They'd planned on having it fixed so nice for her. Looking at it through her eyes, he saw the unfinished fireplace, the rough rounds of tree trunk serving as chairs, the too-small table, the untidy leaf beds, the floor muddy from the last rain. The pot left unscrubbed by the fireplace. Oh, she'd want to turn around and head right back to Pennsylvania now.

But Ma was smiling. Seemed like she couldn't stop smiling, even when she saw the unscrubbed pot.

"Just look how you boys have made do," she said.

She walked to the corner and took down the bark box from its shelf. "This looks real homey," she said, turning it over in her hands. "Did you make it?"

Daniel nodded, too grateful to speak.

"We put fishhooks in it," Will told her. "But you could use it for spices and such."

"I will," said Ma. "And I hope you'll make more. We'll have need of storage, you know."

That reminded Pa that the wagon needed to be unpacked. They had left it back a ways where the trail got too narrow for the wheels to pass.

"Come with me, boys," he said.

The wagon was chock-full of supplies. Trunks that likely held clothing and bed quilts. Barrels and sacks and jugs of foodstuffs. A small sack of seed corn. Ma's cooking pots and spinning wheel. The baby's cradle, the same one each of them had been rocked in. Pa's tools. Daniel was glad to see his old musket, and a new rifle besides. But sorry to find that the horse standing in the wagon's traces was not old Ben.

"Had to trade him for a livelier horse or we'd never have made it over the mountains," Pa said. "This one's named Blaze."

"Where's Trooper?" Will asked.

Pa's face looked even more drawn. "Died last winter," he said shortly. "That old dog would never have made it out here either."

They carried in the foodstuffs first. More cornmeal and white flour and molasses and salt. A large sack of potatoes. A slab of bacon. Even a little tied-up package of sugar.

Bacon, potatoes, sugar!

It had been so long since Daniel had tasted any of them. His stomach was suddenly gnawing with hunger, though he'd just had breakfast.

As they unloaded the wagon, Ma quickly arranged things inside the cabin. Her pots next to the fireplace, the foodstuffs nearby. The cradle on the other side. The girls helped. Zeke trailed after Daniel and Will, trying to help carry things, asking questions every minute.

"Did you see any Indians?

"Where's the schoolhouse?

"Are there wolves like Pa said? And bears? Were you scared?"

Finally Ma shooed them all outside. "I'm going to give the floor a good sweeping," she said.

"Come on," Will said to the younger ones. "We'll show you the creek."

With Zeke and the girls at their heels, Daniel and Will led the way down the path. They pointed out where Will had speared his biggest fish, and fallen into the freezing water. They showed them the fish trap.

Leaning over the bank, Zeke exclaimed, "I see fish!"

Sure enough, two fish were caught inside. "We'll bring them to Ma," Daniel said.

Then they set off to check their rabbit snares.

It was proving to be a good day all around. In the first one he looked at, Will found a fat brown rabbit. It was still alive, twitching slightly, but Will struck it with a heavy stick and it lay still.

"Now Ma can make one of her good stews," he said, grinning. "With wild onion. And potatoes."

Sarah stared at the thin noose around the rabbit's neck. "How did you do that?" she asked.

Will showed her another snare he'd set nearby. "Solomon taught us," he said.

"Solomon?"

"An Indian we met," Daniel answered. "He taught us a lot."

"You *did* meet Indians!" Zeke cried. "Did they have tomahawks? And war paint?"

Daniel shook his head. "It wasn't like that," he said. "Solomon was a friend to us."

So much had happened to him and Will in the past few months, he realized. They had so many stories to tell, about Solomon and all he'd taught them, about the bear, about the snowy winter that seemed like it would never end, and the lucky kill of the deer. And the horse mill. It would take a long time to tell it all.

They gathered greens on the way back to the cabin: wild onion and dandelion and wild mustard.

"Ma!" cried Abby, bursting in the door. "We brought dinner!"

214

Ma looked up from where she sat on a log chair, rocking baby Josiah in his cradle. Her eyes took in the rabbit dangling from Will's hand, the fish, the handfuls of greens.

"Oh, my," she said. "You surely did."

"They have traps!" Zeke told her excitedly. "Rabbit traps and fish traps."

Daniel was surprised to see Ma's eyes filling once more with tears.

"You boys can do so much," she said, her voice choking. "You're pretty near grown."

Then she smiled and wiped her eyes. "I believe I will start cooking," she said, getting to her feet. "Sarah, would you rock the baby? One of you grown boys can skin that rabbit and the other can bring in more firewood."

"Will you make a rabbit stew?" Will asked.

Ma nodded. "And fried fish. And maybe some corn dodgers."

"Hurrah!" shouted Will.

Daniel went out to the woodpile, followed by Zeke.

"I'll help," he offered. "I can carry a big log."

Pa had just finished picketing the horse next to the cabin. "We'll build a shed first thing," he said, "so no varmints can get him."

Unexpectedly he laid his hand on Daniel's shoulder.

"I've been looking over the cabin," he said. "Seems like the chinking stayed in pretty well. You built yourselves a fine woodpile. Appears to me too that you've enlarged the clearing."

"Yes, sir," Daniel answered. "We were about ready to plant."

Pa nodded. "Well, I'm real proud of you boys," he said. "Real proud."

Daniel didn't know what to say. He'd never thought to hear those words coming from Pa.

"We could have done better on the chinking," he said finally. "Some fell out in the winter. And we never got time to finish off the fireplace."

"Never mind." Pa brushed off Daniel's words with a shrug. "You did the best you could."

Daniel couldn't help smiling as he brought in wood for Ma's fire.

It wasn't long before they were all sitting down to her dinner. Pa and Ma and Daniel and Will at the small table, the rest on the floor, eating out of the bowls Will had made. Ma's rabbit stew was just as delicious as Daniel remembered, with chunks of potato and onion in a rich gravy. And some other flavorings he knew from back home. Ma must have brought a few of her herbs with her.

Now, finally, there was time to talk.

Pa started off. "It sure took a lot longer than I figured to get back here," he said with a small smile. "Could be you gave up on ever seeing us again."

Daniel and Will both nodded.

"When I got home to Pennsylvania," he went on, "I found your ma real sick. She took to her bed the day

I got there and couldn't get out of it for weeks. Sarah and Abby tried to take care of her, along with the baby, but it was too much for them.

"Things got so bad, I finally had to take her to her folks outside of Philadelphia. We were there two months. Your grandma and Aunt Sadie nursed her till she got back her strength. We'd just returned to the farm when I was struck down with the same fever."

Ma took up the story then. "Your pa was laid low for another month," she told them. "He kept trying to get up, fretting about you boys, saying we had to get started for Ohio. But then the fever would come back. I kept him down as long as I could, though I was worrying about you too. Then one day he just got out of bed and said, 'We're setting out tomorrow,' and we did. Like as not, he wasn't over it when we left. You can see he's not real strong."

So that was why Pa looked so washed out. Glancing over at him, Daniel thought he seemed strong even so. It wasn't what you saw on the outside. It was something inside Pa that would never let go.

Daniel got to tell their story after that. Not all of it. That would take days more, maybe weeks. But they had days and weeks to finish telling it.

Ma got tearful all over again when she heard about the bear attack. She had to examine Daniel's leg to make sure it was healed right. And Will had to show them his spear.

"I want to kill a bear too!" said Zeke.

"I didn't kill it," Will protested. "Only wounded it some."

"Will you make me a spear?" Zeke pleaded.

No doubt Will would, a small one. And no doubt Zeke would be practicing from now on how he'd kill a bear.

After dinner was over, they lingered, not wanting this time to end.

Daniel looked around the cabin, amazed at how different it looked already. With Pa's guns leaning next to the axe, the trunks and spinning wheel along the wall, Ma's cooking things spread out around the fireplace. Her Bible sitting on the little shelf beside the bark box. She'd soon be reading them stories from it, he could be sure of that. The baby asleep in his cradle, the rest of them gathered round. Yes, this cabin was cozied up almost like home.

Pa was thinking about the cabin too.

"First thing I'll do is lay down a puncheon floor," he said. "You boys can help split the logs. Then we'll fix the roof and put up a sleeping loft and make a stout wood door. And build a bedstead and a bigger table and maybe a bench or some stools."

"Ma will want her window," Daniel reminded him. "With real window glass." He still had that picture in his head of Ma looking out at the little dogwood tree when it bloomed again next spring.

Ma spoke up.

"A window or two would be a mighty fine thing," she said, smiling. "But I can wait awhile for the window glass.

218

Before that we'll need a milk cow. And some chickens. And your pa's got his heart set on a few hogs, if this first crop of corn comes in well."

"We can start planting tomorrow," Pa said. "Thanks to you boys."

They would be busy in the days ahead, Daniel could see that. Planting and fixing up the cabin. Most likely Ma would want help putting in a vegetable garden too. Their first crop of corn might not come in well. He'd seen how things could go wrong out here. They might have to wait awhile for a cow and chickens and hogs. And Ma's window glass could take a real long time. But they'd work hard, together.

Daniel looked over at Will. His eyes were eager, impatient to get started.

"Could be we might drop in some seeds before nightfall," he said.

"Could be," agreed Pa.

Yes, Daniel thought. With a little luck, they'd have a farm.

AUTHOR'S NOTE

This story is based on an actual incident in Ohio history, as recorded in a collection of reminiscences of pioneer life entitled *Historical Collections of Ohio* by Henry Howe. Not much is known about the episode except the two brothers' names and ages and the fact that they survived alone in a partly built cabin in the wilderness for eight months from the fall of 1803 until the spring of 1804. I have had to imagine the rest.

Because this is fiction, I have changed the boys' names. However, I have tried to remain true to the spirit of those sturdy, adaptable families who settled the American west.

ACKNOWLEDGMENTS

I am indebted to Jeff and Judy Kalin of Primitive Technologies, Inc., for their expert advice on nature and survival techniques. And to Joseph Bruchac for his reading of the Native American portions of the manuscript.